"I can't think when you're lying there naked."

Despite the sheet covering her, apparently Luke could tell she wore no nightgown. Well, if the lawman had a problem with that, Roxy had the solution. "So take off your clothes and join me. You can show me your *gun.*" She giggled.

"I don't think that's a good idea." He shifted on his feet where he stood near the motel-room door.

She stretched on the bed provocatively, sticking her legs out from under the sheet.

He put his hand up to his forehead. "You're a dangerous woman."

"So come and give me a ticket."

"For what?" he said, his voice tight.

She lowered the sheet from her shoulders toward her breasts. His eyes followed. It was as if with those deep brown eyes he touched each inch she revealed. "Indecent exposure."

He swallowed. "Actually, I think I'm going to have to take you into protective custody."

"Who will you be protecting me from?"

"Me."

Dear Reader,

I'm so excited to introduce my first book. For me it's both a happy ending and an exciting beginning. When I was writing Roxy's story I knew a flawed yet feisty heroine might be a difficult sell. Fortunately, my editor saw the appeal of a character with a past. Roxy may be a *bad* girl, but she's got a vulnerable heart.

Roxy comes from Dallas and she's got it all—a trust fund with all the trappings. Raised by a staff of servants trying to mold a little redheaded girl into a debutante, she discovered that every act of rebellion got her the attention she craved. As a result, Roxy doesn't hesitate to do anything that occurs to her and damn the consequences. She's been down, but she's never been out. And she's never been in love.

Sheriff Luke Hermann loves his west Texas town. These are his people, and he's always been able to anticipate trouble—until a long-legged gal drives her screaming yellow Porsche right into his heart....

I hope you enjoy this view of my home state of Texas. It would be so exciting to hear from you! You can write to me c/o Harlequin Books, 225 Duncan Mill Road, Don Mills, Ontario M3B 3K9, Canada.

Here's to your own happy ending,

Mara Fox

MARA FOX

I SHOCKED THE SHERIFF

TORONTO • NEW YORK • LONDON
AMSTERDAM • PARIS • SYDNEY • HAMBURG
STOCKHOLM • ATHENS • TOKYO • MILAN • MADRID
PRAGUE • WARSAW • BUDAPEST • AUCKLAND

I dedicate this book to my own hero, Mark Horstman,
who, once upon a time in Hawaii,
sold his surfboards to buy a diamond ring....

ISBN 0-373-69182-3

I SHOCKED THE SHERIFF

This edition published by arrangement with Harlequin Books S.A.

www.eHarlequin.com

Printed in U.S.A.

1

ROXANNE ADAMS RAN her dry tongue over parched lips. *"Damn. I've done it again."*

"Ohh," she said as she raised her head and then rotated her neck. She grabbed the steering wheel in a punishing grip. The smell of vanilla car freshener filled her senses.

This time I'm safe in the Porsche.

Wearily she rested her head on the top edge of the steering wheel. She didn't want to replay the episode from so long ago, but the nightmare scene from her last binge boiled over. The drunken man had lifted his head to tell her what a pretty girl she was. Naked, she'd looked up into his filthy face and had seen a mirror of what she'd become.

That vision kept her sober. That vision, the twelve steps, and all her friends from AA. It'd been over two years.

I can handle this. I can. I have to.

Tears moistened her gritty eyes. Sure, cry, you ninny, she told herself as she rubbed them. But Joey's hanging on. He might have tried to kill himself, but he's gonna get a second chance whether he wants to or not and this time he'll make it.

Roxy groaned, then lifted her head from the steering wheel. She knew if she looked in the mirror there'd be a funny circle imprint on her forehead. It had happened before, more times than she cared to count. Sometimes she'd still been drunk and it had seemed funny, but not today.

Today, she was sober. She felt a cautious sense of elation.

Knocking on the window got her attention. She looked over into the condemning eyes of a man in a familiar uniform. That must have been what had awakened her. Why, oh why, had she driven out here?

But she knew. Driving out here had saved her.

"Open your door, please. I won't ask you again."

What was he going to do about it? Shoot out the windows? Drag her out of the car by her hair? The Porsche was legally registered in her name, a gift of love from her father for staying sober for a whole year. She'd tell this big, bad cop a thing or two...respectfully, of course.

No sense in ending up in a hick holding tank for sassing the local law. No matter how desperate her high school was for teachers, they'd fire her in a heartbeat if they found out she'd spent her summer vacation in a West Texas jail.

Funny, how the youngest person in her AA group had inspired her to use her degree to teach and mentor at the high school. Finding a purpose had helped her to stay sober, and watching over kids who had it rougher made her appreciate her life.

She grinned at the irony, relishing even this nowhere

place and this nobody cop who'd come to rescue her. Wallowing in the sheer relief of being sober.

Roxy unlocked the car doors.

"Step out of the car slowly."

She pushed herself away from the steering wheel. It didn't do any good to argue with certain types of cops—*his* kind of cop. She could tell by the look in his frigid brown eyes.

Still sitting, facing forward, she put one tentative foot outside, grateful for the firmness of the ground and the rustle of dry grass beneath her sandal as a familiar wave of dizziness washed over her.

She breathed deeply, filling her lungs several times before she noticed him shifting in apparent frustration. "I'm sorry, officer. I'm unsteady this morning. Forgot my medication. Ran out of gas. An all-around unhappy morning."

Roxy's tone wasn't flip, but it wasn't placating, she didn't have placating in her soul, no matter how many spectacular mistakes she'd made.

He looked her over as if she were roadkill. He'd likely found less pleasant company on the side of the road, but she guessed he wouldn't admit it. She ran her tongue over her teeth. She hadn't brushed them, but she hadn't been drinking, either. *Lucky for him, my breath won't be too toxic.*

"You think you could pass a Breathalyzer?" he asked.

Of course, a sheriff from Hicksville would assume the worst. She slung the other leg around the edge of the seat. There she sat facing him, feet on the ground, grass tickling her calves. She resisted the urge to tug on her very short shorts. It would just draw attention to her naked thighs. *Out here, anyone not wearing jeans and cowboy boots probably ended up arrested for indecent exposure.*

"I haven't been drinking." She tried on a smile. Flipped a hunk of hair over her shoulder. Let him think whatever he wanted to just as long as he gave her a lift to the nearest gas station with a rest room.

He looked her over. "What kind of medicine?"

He'd obviously been paying attention to more than her lank red hair and the circles under her eyes. Score one for the policeman. "Do you have any orange juice? I'm worried about my blood sugar."

"Are you claiming to be diabetic?" He sounded skeptical.

"I'm borderline diabetic. And I'm out of gas. So I guess I'm going to be riding with you. If you'll help me to my feet we can start for town." Then she remembered. "If there's a town in this godforsaken place."

"You don't even know where you are? Don't you know it's dangerous to run out of gas in West Texas in the middle of the hottest summer on record? In a few hours you'd be cookin' in that car and there's no shade and no water for quite a ways."

She grimaced up at him. This was familiar territory. All cops liked to give lectures. "Actually, I drove all this way just so I could try my hand at hitchhiking along a desert highway in the middle of summer." She brushed her hair back again. "And I think it's unkind of you to deprive me of that scintillating experience."

"That fancy word tells me that you're educated, but you're not very smart. You could have died of heat prostration out here."

Roxy licked her dry lips, imagining being stuck here even more thirsty than she already was. "I guess I just wasn't thinking straight."

She was telling the truth. Her longtime friend Joey had attempted suicide after being dry for six months. The shock had hit her hard and fast. And the five-year-old memory of finding her brother, overdosed on Ecstasy, had followed on its tail, kicking her in the teeth like it was yesterday. She'd felt brittle, an urge away from tumbling headfirst off the wagon.

Instead Roxy had grabbed her keys, driving the loneliest stretches of roads she could find. Anything to avoid the neon lure of civilization and alcohol.

"Ma'am, I need to see your identification. Where're you from?"

"I'm from Dallas. I have my driver's license here somewhere." She reached around to look for her purse and found it wasn't under the seat where she usually stowed it. She looked in the back seat and didn't see it there. In fact the car looked decidedly bare. In her rush to get away she hadn't brought her purse, her phone, or anything else.

"Gosh, darn it!" Swearing was not allowed at school and she cringed at the sound of her silly exclamation. *Too bad it doesn't go with his image of me as a lowlife.* She would have enjoy harassing this hick, if not for her hard-won job.

Roxy turned back and put her feet on the ground again. The fresh air smelled good, but now she caught the faintest scent of warming asphalt. Add lots of exhaust and it'd be just like home. Roxy looked up at him and shrugged. "Sorry, no purse."

"Miss Dallas, you've got no straight answers and no identification?"

"I'm full of straight answers. You just haven't asked me the right questions."

"Okay, I'll bite. Do you usually drive without your license?"

She shrugged. "I was slightly upset when I left home." *Understatement of the century.* "I forgot it."

"You don't leave me with any choice. I'll have to run you into Red Wing and you can sit at the station until we get some confirmation of who you are."

"Red Wing?"

"It's a town about ten miles from here. You're lucky I had business out at Pete's place or you'd have been in a world of hurt. This is a lonely stretch of road."

"Do they have gas pumps and orange juice in Red Wing?"

He nodded.

Roxy didn't know why she bothered being sarcastic. He didn't even notice. It was almost as irritating as his cop attitude. Because he sure was a handsome man under that uniform, with a body good enough to wake her slumbering hormones.

Down, girl. She'd always been a sucker for broad shoulders and a tight little bottom, but the tight-ass attitude belonged to a cop. *It's not hormones. It's just my blood sugar.*

"I'll need your keys so I can lock the car." He looked at her expectantly. It took a minute, but she soon realized he meant for her to get up. She knew she'd never make it to her feet so she held out one hand. "If you don't want to haul my butt out of the grass you'd better help me up. I'm dizzy as all get out."

He took her hand as if it were the last thing he wanted to do. He sure was tall. Once she stood up she had to tilt her head back to look up into his face.

"Thank you." She said it rather reluctantly since it felt like he'd rather be hauling a carcass off of the road.

He didn't seem to notice her attitude for which she was famous. Roxy handed him the keys with a grimace. *Be smart, girl. Don't challenge him. He's not worth getting fired over.*

He nodded, putting the keys in his pocket and one hand on her arm. She tried to pull away, but it only made her more dizzy so she accepted his touch while doing her best to ignore the zing that had all her nerves humming. He walked her to his car as if she were an old woman, towering over her despite her height and the two-inch heels on her sandals.

His impersonal attitude didn't upset her, she told herself. She didn't care if the gorgeous cop from Hicksville saw her as a stray and not as a woman. He probably had a wife and six children back at the ranch.

The only thing that mattered was that she'd done it. Stayed sober despite extreme provocation. It proved... well, it didn't prove anything. Twenty-six years old and she'd still run, still hadn't been strong enough. Over two years sober and she was still afraid.

Terrified.

So I'll just keep fighting it the way I have been—one day at a time. And today's a good day, another day clean. She hummed a little ditty on the way to the police car.

SHERIFF LUKE HERMANN started his car and then pulled out from behind the eye-popping-yellow Porsche. That was a custom paint job if he'd ever seen one. The car was a beaut and so was the woman.

He didn't say anything else to the redheaded woman he'd dubbed Miss Dallas. And not because he was usually tongue-tied around beautiful women. No, this woman didn't count because he was working, and a woman who'd slept in her car should be decidedly unattractive, not long, lean, and lethal.

Luke shook his head.

He couldn't be sure to what extent she'd broken the law, besides not having her driver's license with her. He would soon find out.

"What's your name?" she asked.

Her voice sounded like she'd been chewing gravel or chain smoking for forty years and she didn't look a day over thirty.

He glanced at her. She gave him an affected smile that told him she didn't like cops any more than he liked her. Luke knew she had an attitude a mile wide under her carefully chosen words.

"My name's Sheriff Hermann."

She just nodded and sat silently. Then she leaned back and appeared to go to sleep. His own disappointment startled him. He'd wondered what she might say next. She looked to be full of surprises.

Usually he didn't like surprises. That's why he'd come back to the town he'd grown up in. He knew everyone, their family histories, and their propensity for breaking or bending the law. Usually trouble was a long time brewing and he could anticipate it, prevent it.

Sometimes.

He wasn't a hero, but he protected his own.

So how come the tall gal didn't rouse his protective instincts? Her sassy mouth and all that red hair hit him in a more visceral spot. *Easy, boy. You don't usually do your thinking with your balls.*

She stirred, apparently not asleep after all. "I'll need your name." He shouldn't bother asking—without proper identification she probably wouldn't give him her real name. But it was worth a shot.

"I'm Roxy, Roxanne Adams."

He nodded. Under any other circumstances he might be saying "pleased to meet you," and meaning it.

"You're a woman of few words, Miss Adams."

"Uh-huh."

He shook his head. He hadn't a clue what to do with her. "You feeling okay?"

She rolled her head toward him on the seat. For the

first time he noticed her eyes were blue. As deep and blue as the creek on his fishing property down in Comstock. The whites were clear. It didn't look as if she was recovering from a binge or coming off of a drug high. And she hadn't stolen the car.

This woman fit that car perfectly.

"I'm okay." She turned away from him, slouching deep into the seat, and wedged one knee on the glove compartment.

Luke sneaked a look at her legs. Lord, they went on for a good ways. He didn't even give her heck about putting her knee on his dash. His mouth went dry and he longed to reach for a Dr. Pepper from his stash behind the seat. Tapping on the steering wheel, he wondered how such a tall gal fit those legs into that little car.

While Luke subtly watched her, she dropped into sleep. Roxanne Adams fell asleep as easily as a child, like she had an off switch. She had a fine body to go along with those long legs. He was chagrined that he noticed the way her seat belt hugged her high, rounded breasts.

She's trouble. Because he was thinking about her all wrong. *But she isn't the kind of trouble I have to worry about. I'll just drop her off at the clinic and she can be someone else's problem.* He pulled his eyes away from her and tried to focus on the road. But every time she gave a little sigh he felt it tug at something deep inside.

He hated misjudging people. And lately Luke had begun to wonder if the job was hardening him. Here he was treating this woman as if she'd done something wrong, because she stirred him. What was he supposed to do with a woman who talked hard but slept like a defenseless child with her hair curling around her face?

He pulled into the small clinic, which served the town in emergencies. Then he gently shook her awake. The pallor of her skin made a sprinkle of golden freckles stand out like bits of brown sugar all across her nose.

He watched the dawning awareness in her eyes with regret. For a moment she'd been sleepy—vulnerable. Then she recognized him and her expression hardened. She *had* been in trouble before. He'd let those long legs distract him. He should have been angry that he'd given her the benefit of the doubt; instead it made him curious.

Roxanne blinked and sat up. She looked out the car window. "Oh, shi...shoot. A clinic. The only thing worse than a clinic is the police station."

"Seen your share of holding pens?" he asked.

She swung her head in his direction. A hint of a smile lurking around her mouth. "Not for a long time. What gave me away?"

"I've seen your type before."

She turned away. "That's the problem with cops' *types*. They can't see past the stereotypes to the person."

Luke didn't acknowledge the direct hit to his ego. He always tried to be fair, but after years in law enforcement, the criminals wore you down. You trusted your instincts less and your experience more, and because he didn't want her to be a criminal, he'd broken all of his own rules.

"Nothin' you want to say?" she asked, rubbing her hand over her face.

That childlike gesture made him wonder. He shored up his cynicism and shook his head.

"I should call my father. He'll be worried."

"Miss Adams, I'll help you get in touch with your father once we're inside." *Let the doc have her. He'll tell me if she's got a medical problem or a habit.*

She nodded. "Probably a good idea to deal with my blood sugar first so I'm coherent when I call him, otherwise he'll be on his plane in a heartbeat."

He wondered what it would be like to have a private plane at your disposal. Was being rich what made her so sassy?

"Then I guess we're going in. Is it going to be a needle?" She rubbed her arm as if already feeling the sting.

"A test."

"A drug test?" Her eyebrow arched above her eye.

Her eyebrow matched the shade of her hair. He would have expected her to be a fake. But it seemed that her vibrant hair color was natural. "A blood sugar test."

She rewarded him with a perfect smile that hit him in the gut like a fist. "Fancy that, a blood sugar test. I figured ya'll still used horse piss and leeches."

He turned away, busying himself with opening his door, determined she wasn't going to get a rise out of him. He looked over when he heard the opposite door open.

She stepped out on her side but once on the sidewalk she swayed like tall grass in a storm. He stepped around the front of his vehicle and when he reached her side he grasped her shoulders with his hands. "I've got ya."

Roxanne Adams tried to step away from him. "The hell you do. I can walk into the clinic. I'll just tell my body I'll reward it with orange juice if it walks just those few steps. You do have orange juice?"

Luke squashed his appreciation of her grit and the lust those long, lean curves inspired. She needed him. "I insist on helping you. I don't want you to sue Doc Peterson if you land on the sidewalk on your head."

"Really, Officer, I'm fine," she protested, literally trying to stand her ground.

He just propelled her along, one of the benefits of being taller and stronger than even the tallest of the fair sex. "I'll help you. We wouldn't want you to fall down and get bruises. You might claim police brutality was involved."

"Brutality? Like your grip on me? Are you afraid I'll go running off and get lost in the crowds?" She gestured toward the almost empty street where Mrs. Henderson walked her ancient dog and three kids rode bikes.

He grinned and loosened his grip just a little.

She smiled back easily enough. So why did he get the impression those smiles were a rare occurrence?

"I'd never claim you'd been anything other than downright decent...for a cop."

Luke's experience said she wasn't someone he should stick his neck out for, yet his instincts said otherwise. And his body clamored. But Roxanne Adams was trouble any way you looked at her. And he had to consider Carla, his longtime girlfriend.

Suddenly Roxy went limp in his arms. An unusual sense of alarm thrummed through him. He'd been tested in many different kinds of situations, but this felt different. He gently scooped her up and carried her into the clinic, wishing he knew what kind of trouble they were headed for.

"WHAT ARE YOU LOOKING AT?" Her voice couldn't sustain the intended irascibility. But her eyes burned at him.

He wondered how her parents slept at night worrying about her. He hadn't been able to squash his unease while waiting to discover what was wrong with her and it had made him testy. "I think I'm lookin' at roadkill."

"Such a nice sentiment. Are all country boys so poetic?"

She thinks I'm a hick. That should ease the ache in my loins.

Yet he wondered. Why was he in this hick town? Suddenly he could see it through her eyes and he wondered if it was small-town inertia holding him in Red Wing. The reassurance of familiar places and people. *I really need to see Carla.* He'd been going out with his lady for several years, and today he couldn't remember the fragrance of her perfume.

And yet, all day he'd been remembering the smell of the vanilla air freshener in the Porsche. "Well, Miss Dallas, us hicks managed to patch you up without the leeches and horse piss."

"Patch me up? Is that what you call it?"

"I take it you're not feeling much better."

She widened her eyes. "I guess not."

"When was the last time you stopped for something to drink? You were really dehydrated. They gave you a shot big enough for a horse."

"That's probably all they have in this one-horse town."

He shook his head. "Not really a big shot. Just the IV in your arm for a couple of hours. You were conscious, talking, but sleepy. Don't you remember?"

She pushed her hair off of her face. "I remember the doctor talking to me but not much he said. I sleep like a dead person."

"You *were* pretty out of it."

"Did you wait so you could take me down to the station when I woke up? Are you desperate for company? Can't be too many women in this town under eighty."

"Is there any reason for me to take you down to the station?" He looked at her intently. "You got anything you want to confess?"

"You've got a sense of humor like a mortician. Come to think of it I do remember having nightmares. I think you featured in a few of them."

As if to prove her wrong, he gave her a charming smile. "I just stuck around to make sure you didn't cause any trouble."

"Ah, Farmer John is concerned about everyone but

the unfortunate woman stranded on the side of the road because of a medical condition. Your sympathy is astounding." She struggled to sit up, clutching the neck of the hospital gown choking her. These stupid things had all the material up-front.

He put out his hands like he was trying to turn a stampeding horse. "Whoa. You best lie back down. I don't think the good doctor is ready for you to be getting up." His hands hung in the air just above her chest as if he were afraid she might be contagious.

"I gotta pee, Farmer John, and there ain't no way I'm gonna let them hook me up to any catheter. Those things hurt like hell." She grabbed the railing, pulling herself to a sitting position.

He took a step back.

She finally made it to her feet.

Then she grimaced. *Easy does it.* But she wouldn't make it if the floor didn't stay in one place. She muttered a mild expletive under her breath. Wouldn't want to shock the sheriff.

He didn't say anything. In fact his silence seemed almost strained. She took two leg-shaking, strength-rattling steps and then she looked back over her shoulder.

His gaze was riveted on her naked hind end.

She gave him a faint smile and a salute, which had him blushing the color of a police light. Apparently he didn't like being caught in the act. Too bad he couldn't give her a ticket for indecent exposure.

The door to her room slammed shut as the sheriff made his getaway.

She waddled the remaining steps to the bathroom. Nothing like a man with his mouth hanging open to give a woman a boost.

2

"WHAT WAS TED DOING IN HERE?" Sheriff Hermann gestured toward the man who'd just walked out of her room with a clipboard.

"He's desperately in love with me, but he's really not my type." Roxy smiled as she finished slipping into her sandals. The way the sheriff had run out on her she'd have bet quite a sum on him never coming back. Seemed he had more gumption than she'd given him credit for, or maybe he was interested in seeing her hind end again.

"I guess you're feeling better. You want to tell me what Ted wanted or do I have to go and ask him?"

She sighed. Was he always so impatient? "He's the checkout committee. I'm releasing myself and they don't want to be responsible."

He didn't look at her. Instead he seemed to be focusing on the insipid wallpaper above her head. "I heard you made quite a fuss."

Fuss was her middle name. When her governess had tried to mold her into being a debutante destined for an advantageous marriage, she'd rebelled, doing and saying most anything that occurred to her.

"Have you come to take me to the police station,

Farmer John?" Her voice sounded just as steady and offhanded as she wanted it to. Let him think he intimidated her by hanging around with his uniform buttoned up tight enough to choke him. "Is it a crime to want to avoid spending the night in a hospital?"

He put a hand up to his badge. "They usually just release people when they're ready. It's not really a hospital, just a clinic. But they've got to be careful with out-of-town folks."

"You just can't trust anyone these days," she told him flippantly.

"The doc was trying to do you a favor, Miss Dallas." The sheriff looked at her earnestly. "You weren't clear-headed enough to wire for money until after the bank closed. Where're you planning to sleep?"

"Are you taking me to the station or not?" Roxy demanded.

He'd looked at her insurance card when they'd gone out to get her car. Her legal papers had been in the glove compartment and up-to-date. He'd found nothing illegal. "How many times are you going to ask me? You didn't break any laws. You just got sick. The doc said that between the dehydration and the low blood sugar you probably weren't thinking too clearly."

"You reckon?" Sarcasm all but dripped from her tongue.

He didn't seem to notice. "So there's no reason to take you to the station."

She surged to her feet. "Darn right."

"I just thought I'd come by and see if you need a ride

to the Cozy Daze Motel. You can get a clean room until you're ready to leave town."

She took a couple of steps closer to him. He had great shoulders, great chest but too much cop attitude.

Still, it was fun to rile him, or have him blushing like a choir boy over a little flesh. And she definitely felt better. "You in a hurry to see me leave town? You don't want me to stick around and see the...sights?"

"I think you'll be on your way home real soon. But I realize you don't have your purse with you. I thought I could help you if you need some funds."

"Funds? Ain't that a bit formal?" She sidled right up next to him, rolling her hips as she walked. "You offering me bed and board?"

His cheeks pinkened. "I'm offering you a loan until you get some money from home."

"How am I gonna get some money? I don't even have a credit card or a check." She leaned in closer.

He nodded. "I'll help you."

"Why?" She touched the top button on his uniform.

He stepped back from her as if her touch burned him. "I figure you need a hand. You don't know anyone in town."

"I don't know *you.* And this morning you looked at me as if I were slime crawling out from under a rock. Now you're just dying to send me back me to where I belong. Am I so dangerous?"

"I didn't look at you as if you were slime. I didn't want you to die in the heat. It was one-hundred-thirteen degrees out there today. I was doing my job."

She took the step he'd put between them. This time his lips tightened, yet he stood his ground. She smiled. She reached up and touched a bead of sweat on his brow. His dark hair waved temptingly just above where she touched him. She took a deep breath. He smelled like sweat and something else. Something manly. "I guess it's...hot."

He didn't budge, even when she rubbed her bare leg against his trouser leg. But he licked his lips. His nostrils flared as if he was catching her scent, as well. "It's hot all right."

She hoped he couldn't feel her leg trembling. She hadn't felt the flare of honest desire in a long time. Hadn't allowed herself to stray off course. A course chosen for self-preservation. Seemed he might be more dangerous to her than she to him.

"You saved me...." This time her voice shook. He threw her off balance. Made her feel things.

"I was just doing my job." It came out husky. His eyes slid down the length of her body.

She abruptly pulled away. She didn't need the distraction of an affair right now. She needed to get her head on straight. "Your job's done, Farmer John. Don't worry about me. I put in a call to my father. He's going to wire money and some paperwork to the Goat Herder's Bank of West Texas. I'll be moving along before I can infect your town with my evil ways."

"It's Ranchers Security Bank." He sounded angry.

She went to the side of the bed and collected her sunglasses. "Yeah? I'll remember that when I go looking for the right bank. This town probably has a slew of banks to choose from. I'll bet you folks even got a Wal-Mart and a laundry called Duds and Suds, or something equally charming."

"At least we don't have to send for Daddy's money to bail us out when we're irresponsible." His voice sounded mild. "And we don't have a Wal-Mart."

It took her a moment to feel the sting.

"I guess you never had to call Daddy to bail you out of trouble."

"Not since I was fifteen years old."

"Yeah? Well I'm not so perfect. In fact I'm amazingly full of flaws. You name the mistake and I've made it. My dad might be a very busy lawyer, but these days he makes me a priority. Even if I need bailing out like a fifteen-year-old."

"He must have some patience."

She remembered how her father would set her on his lap when she'd been in trouble, and patiently explain why she was supposed to listen to her governess. "He does."

"Then you shouldn't go out of your way to worry him."

Roxy smiled. Worrying her father had been the only way to get his attention back in those days. "I didn't do it on purpose." *At least not this time.* "And I can take care of myself. You don't have to worry about anything. Your little ole town is safe from big bad me. I have no intention of staying more than a day or two."

"Good. I don't know if Red Wing can stand the excitement. But I'll drive you over to the Cozy Daze."

"That's okay. Apparently my car's at Larry's gas station, right down the street. I'm grateful you had it towed into town. I'll just walk over there and get it."

"It's hot out there."

"I'm from Dallas. It's hot there, too."

"It's still over ninety degrees."

She looked at him in honest surprise. "Really? I thought it'd be cooler."

"My tires sucked at the road as I drove in—asphalt's still oozy from the heat."

"Find anything interesting out there? Coyotes, scorpions, stranded women?"

"Nope. You're the only one today. Do you want a ride or not?"

"I guess so." She ran her hands over the front of her shorts. Why did she suddenly feel so vulnerable? Was it because she didn't want to rely on anyone? Especially not him? "What day of the week is it?" She tugged on a long lock of hair hanging over her shoulder. Let him scoff about her disorientation. She'd fillet him.

Farmer John didn't scoff. "It's Thursday. The bank will be open first thing in the morning."

She smiled faintly. What would he say if he knew how many times she'd lost track of the date? Whole weeks had disappeared in an alcoholic stupor. If he knew he'd walk away from her in disgust.

Without another word he turned and walked out of the room. She followed. The two people on duty ignored them as they went by. It didn't surprise her. It was unlikely she was the only one who'd objected to spending the night. If Farmer John was any indication, they grew them hardheaded in this part of the county.

He opened the door of the cruiser for her and held it open like he was escorting her on a date. She couldn't help but smile at him. "Thank you, Sheriff."

He smiled. "You're welcome, Miss Adams."

She settled herself amongst all the technology, radios and other cop things. Then, when he sat down beside her she admonished him. "Call me Roxy."

He shook his head.

"Do you prefer Farmer John or do you intend to be formal? Didn't your parents give you a first name?"

"I'm always professional when I'm doing my job," he said, ignoring the rest of her comment.

"I thought you were doing me a favor. It's after hours. Or are you checking up on me? Did you put my name on the list or something?" Her voice rose.

"No, this is just a favor to someone from out of town. I didn't do a records search on you, because you didn't break the law. However, right this moment you don't have a car or any money, so I thought you might accept a helping hand. Graciously."

"You expect me to be gracious when you won't even tell me your name?" She turned away tugging on her hair, unwilling to show her relief that he didn't know about her record. Even though it wasn't much more than a couple of drunk and disorderly charges. Drunks were usually content to hurt themselves and her daddy had enough money to smooth her way.

"My name's Luke."

Grateful, she turned from those ugly memories and smiled at him. "See, Luke, that wasn't so hard."

"Are you always like this?"

Roxy put a hand to her heart with a dramatic flourish. "Oh, my goodness, he told me his name," she teased him. "His reputation as a hard-hearted sheriff's ruined forever."

He flushed again.

His ability to flush might be endearing, but she wasn't letting him off the hook so easily. "I might have to rent some space on a billboard. I'll tell the town what a marshmallow you really are."

"You'd have trouble finding a spare billboard in this town."

Luke looked downright human when he fought a grin, which was good enough for her.

She turned to study the town. The buildings around them were a hodgepodge of materials and styles, some were stucco and others brick. A few stood vacant with boards where the windows would have been. Others appeared to be closed up for the night. She spotted a convenience store and a restaurant with a line of trucks in the parking lot.

She guessed the taverns must be out of the city limits. There were no neon cocktails flashing on the side of the road. She remembered Joey with a jolt of pain. It was just as well the taverns were out of reach.

"You people really do roll up the streets at sundown."

"We like it quiet."

He turned west and the sky was on fire with the setting sun. She sucked in her breath at the glory of it. "It's magnificent."

"Yeah. It's pretty. With no skyscrapers or trees to block the sky you can literally see for miles. This part of the country is known for its big skies. Just wait till the stars come out."

He pulled into a small motel.

A small thrill of alarm swept through her. "I figured we'd go and get my car." She pulled a piece of hair around to rub against her cheek.

"I'll deliver it tomorrow. You look tired."

"I'm not tired. I slept all day." She put her hand up to cover the yawn that threatened to give her away. "I feel naked without my car."

Roxy couldn't see if he was blushing again, or if it was the light from the sunset coloring his face. She hated this mushy, vulnerable feeling. Who was he? Why did he make her feel as if he could cleanse her tarnished soul with his innocence?

The ability to blush is no indication of innocence. He's probably had his share of binges and women. Get a hold of yourself. You're just tired and sick.

She flinched when he reached over as if to touch her face. "I don't know what you're thinking, but I can tell you're not feeling great."

"How?"

"Your freckles get darker when you're feeling poorly."

She covered her nose. "It's not polite to point out a woman's flaws. I don't have any makeup with me."

He grinned. "You don't need any makeup."

It went straight to her gut.

He left her sitting with her mouth open when he got out of the car. Slowly she followed him, wondering what had just happened. Did Sheriff Luke Hermann have a soft spot for women with freckles?

Luke went into the lobby of the motel. Through the window she could see him conversing with an older man. Rubbing her hands on the front pockets of her shorts, Roxy turned to watch the fading glory of the sunset.

It felt strange to be sober and still have no resources. She didn't want to rely on Luke, or anyone. Once she checked out of the clinic, she'd planned to turn off on a side road and sleep in her car. She just couldn't spend the night in the clinic. The smell of the place brought back some really bad memories.

I can pay him tomorrow when the money comes. She didn't suppose she had any choice. And if he'd found her in her car tomorrow he might have done that records search after all. She didn't know if she could have faced him if he'd discovered she'd been hauled into jail.

Mostly to dry out. But no decent person could understand the life she'd led before. Especially not Farmer John.

He'd never understand the struggle she faced daily,

taking her life a day at a time. He was far too perfect to understand someone as flawed as her. Even if he liked freckles.

"Lloyd put you in room fourteen. He says you can use the pool anytime. Just use your key to open the privacy gate."

Grateful to have her back to him, Roxy regained her composure. "Thank you. I'm looking forward to getting a good night's sleep." She finally turned to face him. He stood, illuminated in the fading light. Her own eyes were full of shadows.

"It's over here, near the end. He only has the fifteen units. There's a pool beside the last one."

She followed him down a sidewalk lined with cactus. She watched his buttocks move beneath his pants as he strode along on those long masculine legs of his. *Watch it, girl! Those attributes just happen to belong to a cop.*

They passed three cars lined up outside the doors. A neon sign above them flashing a dancing cactus in verdant green lent the building an unearthly quality.

As Roxy brushed past the sheriff to look beyond the end of the building, she ignored the tingle of awareness and the heat coming off of him. The huge neon sign sat primarily above the fenced pool area. She couldn't see the pool for the high privacy fence shielding it from the highway.

She looked back over her shoulder and gestured toward the sign. "I'll bet all that neon gives the pool some interesting ambience. How far are we from Roswell?"

Luke stood stubbornly in front of the room. "That

sign can be seen for miles and miles. It's probably a godsend for travelers who think there's not another town till El Paso."

"There isn't. This place doesn't qualify as a real town." Roxy headed back.

"You should be grateful there's a town. You'd be coyote bait if I hadn't found you."

She didn't look back. She just stood at the door of room fourteen. She wondered if she should invite him in and then throw him out. It was a tempting thought. He needed to be taken down a few pegs.

"What? No gushing gratitude?" he asked as he stopped next to her in front of the room. He handed her the key with a plastic cactus hanging from it.

"The owners of the motel overdid the desert theme," she commented, figuring it was a safe topic. She couldn't imagine why she'd want to invite him in unless her illness had caused temporary insanity. Roxy just wanted him gone. "I'll bet you the room is orange."

"I'd lose. I think Lloyd's color blind. He always wears the same shade of brown."

Roxy blinked. "Isn't there a Mrs. Lloyd to help him with the color scheme?"

"Naw, she moved to Laredo. I guess she doesn't like small towns, either."

Roxy tried to concentrate on opening the door. How awkward to be standing in front of a motel room with a man she hardly knew. A place where strangers went to be intimate.

Her normally clever fingers fumbled with the key.

Everything external went away when he gently took the key from her hand. Her fingers tingled from the contact. He felt so masculine looming over her, making her feel a sense of security—and an unaccustomed hunger. His strong hands took hold of the knob. Her breath caught, then released in the rhythm of his actions. Her body hummed to a tune she hadn't heard in over two years.

She licked her lips as he fit the key into the lock.

Could he feel it? The air thickened. Everything stood still. Storm weather. Would it be slow and easy when he touched her or would all hell break loose?

With agonizing patience he slid the key home.

She blinked. How had he mesmerized her with so simple an action?

"The lock's sticking."

Roxy bit her lip to hold back a giggle. What would he think if he sensed what was going through her head? That she'd invite him into this room, into her bed, if he showed the slightest interest. And she wouldn't even think of throwing him out.

A man she didn't know. Hadn't she changed at all? "I guess so."

"Are you feeling dizzy again?"

Yes. "No, I'm fine. Just tired."

Prolonged celibacy caused her reaction, she knew. Nothing more.

He didn't move. The tempest hovered just beyond them. If this was big-sky country she should be able to see what came next.

She shifted nervously. He bent down. She closed her eyes. Did she feel the brush of his lips on her cheek? Her eyes popped open. "You didn't kiss me, did you?" she accused him in a tone laced with panic. "I haven't brushed my teeth."

It must be the odd light, Luke thought. Her skin had taken on the washed out color of a corpse, which had brought to mind that stupid fairy tale about a dead girl who needed a kiss.

"I wouldn't kiss you," he denied, hoping he wasn't blushing because he *had* been thinking about her in that way. Not as just a stranger in trouble, but as a woman. "It wouldn't be professional. I just brushed a strand of hair off of your cheek."

Roxanne Adams pursed her lips, as if she didn't think much of him.

Luke laughed at the look on her face. He couldn't seem to help it. She'd looked both horrified and defiant. How he admired her sassy attitude! And despite lank hair, the circles under those crystal eyes and the hitch in her stride, she was desirable. Though she made it clear she didn't want anything to do with him, he wanted her and he wanted to protect her.

What had gotten into him? Hadn't she been making a mockery of his town and his life all day long? Hadn't she shaken his confidence in what he thought he wanted—Carla and a bunch of kids growing up in Red Wing?

Definitely not a ragged redhead with a chip on her shoulder.

"I get the impression this job persona is everything to you. Too bad there isn't a heart under the badge."

Obviously cutting truth was her weapon of choice. Luke simply wouldn't allow her to get to him. "You've been out of your head the entire time you've known me. You're hardly in a position to say anything about me." It came out as casually as he could have wished.

"True. But I'm observant. I'll bet you have no life beyond the job." She ran her tongue over her pale pink lips. "Boy, I'd kill for a drink of water."

She wanted a drink of water? Miss Dallas had just reached inside of his head and summed up his entire life, and she wanted a drink of water?

He blinked. No. She didn't know him, and she didn't know about Carla. *But I can't remember if Carla has freckles under her makeup. And I can't remember if her bottom lip quivers when she's defensive. But I can list the criminal offences of all the men I've arrested and the dates they get out of prison.* When had the job become his life?

He pushed the door open, suddenly needing to get away from her.

She ducked inside.

Luke glanced around. "It's probably not what you're used to, but Millie's floors are clean enough to eat off of."

She walked inside and then reached over to turn on the bedside light. She looked around with a smile. "It's definitely brown. Not much better than orange but better than sleeping outside tonight."

In the soft lighting, her red-gold curls resembled a

crown. What would they look like spread out on the pillows? And her skin? Only a shade darker than the sheets, was it as soft as it looked?

"Who's Millie?" she asked as she bent over to take off her sandals. Her position emphasized her long body.

His gaze clung to the seductive curve of her hip. His feet refused to enter the room. "Millie, the maid who's worked at the motel for twenty plus years. She's also in charge of the town grapevine."

"Ah, gossip. It must be really juicy in a town like this one. Every once in a while someone must run over an armadillo. I'll bet it keeps you folks talking for months."

"This town has its moments."

She approached the doorway where he hung on to the frame. She didn't appear to be in a hurry to get a drink of water. In fact she looked like she had all the time in the world.

Did Carla move like that? Like she was honey in motion? He shifted nervously, wanting to be anywhere but here.

"What moments? Vandalism? Ice cream missing from the town's soda shop?"

For a moment he floundered, wondering what she was talking about, distracted by her every gesture, and then he remembered. Crime. They were talking about his work. The work he never forgot. "Real crimes," he insisted.

She leaned in the shadows of the door frame, her

long, long legs and elegant red toenails inches from his boots.

Luke swallowed hard. "The porch light must be out. I'll go and tell Lloyd. Good night, Miss Adams."

"Aren't you going to tell me about the awful crimes people in this town commit?'

Her eyes were deep and mysterious. He expected they would be mocking if he could see them more clearly. He would do well to remember she's Miss Dallas. "Anywhere there's people there's crime. The sad thing about small towns is that most of the crimes are committed by people who know one another."

"Crimes of passion?"

Her throaty tone reached parts of him he'd do better to ignore. He straightened up. "I've got to be going. Are you going to be okay?"

"Yeah. I'm going to be just fine. Maybe a little lonely."

He reached into his pocket and pulled out two twenty-dollar bills. "This is for whatever you may need until the bank opens tomorrow." He hoped she'd swallow her pride and take the money.

She hesitated. "It's just a loan. Just until the wire comes through," she confirmed.

"Sure."

She took the money and stuffed it into the back pocket of her shorts. He focused on her face but it wasn't much safer than her curves.

"I saw the restaurant. What is it, The Golden Pig? Will you accept a nice dinner in lieu of interest?"

"It's The Golden Pan." His tone had hardened.

"The Golden Pan," she repeated tentatively, uncertainties making her look as innocent as a child.

She hadn't meant to make fun of the restaurant, Luke realized. *I guess I don't have to be so defensive. It's just that it's such a temptation to see her again.*

Too much of a temptation. "You can drop the money by the station if I don't see you before you leave town. Just leave it with Bertha at the front desk."

All too aware he was trying to say goodbye, his gaze touched each of her features.

"Would you like to come in?" She hesitated a moment as if she'd like to take the offer back, shifting nervously on her feet. Then she looked into his face. "I may be from Dallas, but I don't say that to every man I meet," she said defensively.

She trembled when the back of his fingers grazed her soft, flushed cheek. Her eyes were as deep as his fishing hole. Was this why he believed in her? This vulnerability that seemed so honest in a woman so bold and brassy? *She's such a contradiction.*

Such a temptation.

"I can't."

She smiled. "Of course. It's unprofessional. I understand." She almost taunted him.

"I can't because I'm engaged."

Her head came up.

She searched his face. "Thank you for telling me. I'm sorry I've embarrassed myself."

"Don't be embarrassed. It's been a hell of a day and you're not thinking straight."

She nodded. Then she lowered her head. She reached for the door to close it. "Good night."

At the last minute he put his hand up to stop the door from completing its swing. He reached out but didn't touch her this time. "You shouldn't be embarrassed."

She nodded. Not looking at him. It was as if she was ashamed and only wanted him to disappear.

"I've never been more tempted."

3

THE PHONE STARTLED HER out of a nightmare and her hand shook as she reached for the receiver. She pressed it hard against her ear, "Hello?" she rasped out.

"Roxy? Is that you?"

Roxy's heart sank. "Yeah, Mick, it's me. How did you find me?"

"Your dad's housekeeper told me where you were staying. She told me you're sick." Panic sharpened his voice.

"I'm not sick. I just got dehydrated and my blood sugar was low. I'm fine now. Where are you? Are you straight?"

"How could I be? You know what Joey did to himself."

The panic became pain.

"He's going to be all right."

"He did it deliberately. He just couldn't handle it anymore. I'm so tired of fighting this, Roxy. I'm tired of being alone. I want someone to take care of me for a change. Someone strong enough to rely on or I'm outta here."

Roxy nodded. She could understand being tired of fighting. There'd been many days when the siren song of alcohol had been almost too much to bear and death had seemed easier. The course both her mother and her brother had taken when their addictions had overwhelmed them.

She'd also needed someone to turn to, but Roxy would allow no one to help until that terrible morning when she'd hit rock bottom. She'd finally called her father begging for help, and he'd been there for her.

"Roxy?"

She struggled to sit up, grasping the phone in a death grip. "I'm here, Mick."

"I need you to come home. I'm falling into the pit." Obviously stoned, he sobbed without restraint.

"What are you doing? Booze or pills? Mick?"

"Both, man. What does it matter? I'm gonna end up like Joey and I don't care. Better sooner than later."

"Mick? Just tell me where you are."

"I'm at Club Med. Where do you think I am?" His husky voice suddenly sounded sly.

Roxy grasped the phone tighter. "Mick? Tell me where you are." She couldn't go from bar to bar. The lights, the booze, the lure of the only true escape would suck her down.

Especially with the specter of Joey hanging over her. He'd been doing so well and then he'd just given in; he'd gotten drunk, added the right pills. She'd been so frightened. Suddenly she was back in time, cradling her dead brother, David, whose beautiful eyes were glazed in death. Dead by his own hand at twenty-six.

His flesh had been so cold... That scene had stolen a

childhood of wonderful memories. So she tried never to think about David at all.

At least Joey was alive.

"Mick, please, tell me where you are!" Her voice echoed in the empty motel room.

"Damn him." The pain in Mick's voice touched Roxy's heart. The desperation in it touched her soul.

Mick and his brother were really close. They owned a bar. They'd fed her when she'd been so far down she couldn't hold a job and wouldn't go to her father for money. They'd given her a job and self-respect. Then after she'd gotten sober they'd both talked about selling the business, about getting straight. Joey who was forty, ten years older than his brother, had been leading the way.

Roxy knew exactly how Mick felt.

She'd also looked up to David, the way her students looked up to her. That was another reason she couldn't go back. She ran a support group. Those kids deserved better than to have their mentor fall apart.

Look at me, she thought. *I'm no better than Mick.* Hot tears covered her face. "Mick, you're so lucky. He's still alive. Joey's still alive and he's going to be okay."

"I'm lucky? I sure don't feel lucky. I'm trying, Roxy, but why fight it? Joey was stronger than me and he couldn't do it. Why should I even try?"

She heard him take a deep breath.

"I'm sorry I called." He sounded as if her grief had sobered him. "You deserve more than a bum like me for a friend. I should be thinking about you. I'd do anything for you and that includes getting the hell outta of your life. Meanwhile I'm going to get so strung out I won't even remember I had a brother."

"Mick!"

But only the buzz of the dial tone answered her desperate query. She put the receiver down and curled into a ball, shivering, like she would never be warm again.

She had to go to him.

Where will you find him? He'll hide until he's too stoned to remember he's hiding.

She'd find him if she had to search every bar in Dallas. She had a responsibility to help another alcoholic. She couldn't fail him when so many people had been there to help her. She'd find him even if she ended up picking up a drink.

And then you'll die.

The shivering turned to outright shaking.

The shaking continued. She recognized the voice of reason. This part of Roxy knew she wouldn't survive another binge. It wasn't even the diabetes. It was the threat of finding herself at the bottom. If she ever went down to that place again she couldn't come back up.

The phone rang again. She picked it up, hoping Mick had come to his senses. "Hello?"

"Roxy?"

"Daddy, it's me." She rubbed a lock of hair against her cheek.

"What's wrong?" he asked. "You sound terrible, but you told me they had the diabetes under control."

She sniffed, "Mick just called me."

He paused for a moment. "I figured he might. I'm sorry, honey. Mrs. Petty gave him your number at the motel because he said it was an emergency. She thought it was okay because Joey's in your AA group."

"Daddy, he was really stoned. I have to come home and find him. Before he hurts himself."

"I don't think that's a good idea."

"I know. But..."

"I'll find him, Roxy. You stay where you are. We've gotten three calls from the drunks you used to run with."

"He's not like them." She knew she sounded defensive.

"I understand, but he's going to hurt you, Roxy. You can't allow him to depend on you. He has to help himself. You understand better than anyone." The pain of having tried to help her and failed was there in his voice. The pain of a man who'd let his work consume him until he'd lost his wife to alcoholism, and his son to drug addiction and suicide.

It represented another chunk of guilt she had to bear. Her responsibility to Mick warred with her need to atone to her father for the years of heartache he'd endured.

What am I going to do? "I should come home. Joey and Mick need me." She knew her tone lacked conviction.

"No. Just stay put. You ran because you knew you couldn't handle your grief for David and Joey. I know this brought it all back." He sounded as if he was working to keep his own emotions in check.

"I love you, Daddy."

"I love you, too. And I worry about you. This is too much at one time. Joey isn't out of the hospital and he'd want you to do whatever you needed to stay straight. I'll handle Mick." The desperation in his voice convinced her more than anything he said.

"What will you do about Mick?" She sniffed again. Roxy felt guilty about abandoning Mick. His suffering touched more than her sense of responsibility, it touched her heart. He'd sounded so alone.

"I'll find him. I'll look all night long if I have too. Honey, I promise. I'll find him and keep him safe. I'll call someone from your AA emergency list and let them baby-sit him once I've got him."

She took a deep breath, thinking. "Call Michelle, Bubba Watkins, or Houston Sharp. All of them reach out to other alcoholics; they'll understand what he's going through." She couldn't explain any further. Her dad knew why. Everything she knew about her friends from AA she kept confidential. Just as they guarded her ugliest secrets.

"I'll call them. I'll call you back if I can't reach any of them and need more names. Roxy, I promise to take care of this and I'll even visit Joey so he knows how much you wished you could be there for him."

She no longer felt torn by her responsibilities. God willing, there would be other times, when she was stronger, when she could do the reaching out. "Thank you, Daddy. I feel better."

"I love you. I'll send you the two thousand first thing

in the morning. Do you need anything else? Should I ask one of your AA friends to come and stay with you?"

"No, I think it might be good for me to be alone. It'll give me some time to think."

"If you need me I can be there in just a few hours. There has to be a municipal airport nearby."

He sounded worried for her, but she knew he'd accept whatever decision she made. He'd learned long before she'd started drinking that she had to make her own choices, live with her own mistakes. She'd never been a model child.

Every time he'd forced her to do anything it had been a disaster. She'd fought him with every ounce of her will. Until the last binge. Then she'd gone crawling to him for help and he'd been there. He knew things about her that would make any parent cringe with horror. But no matter what other mistakes he'd made as a parent, he'd been there when it counted. She loved him for that.

"I'm really okay. What you've already done is more than enough. Thank you."

"I want to do more for you, Roxy. What else can I do to help?"

"Like I told you when I called from the hospital, I just had to get out of Dallas. That's all. Everything reminded me. I didn't go for a drink, just a long drive. Do you understand, Dad?"

"Yes, and I'm so proud of you."

He sounded choked up. It made her eyes flow again.

"I love you, Daddy."

"I'll call you when the dust settles. Take care of yourself, baby."

"Don't worry, Daddy. I can't get in too much trouble in this hick town."

ROXY SCRAMBLED OUT OF BED. Her head throbbed from crying, her eyelids felt like sandpaper against her eyes. Her nightmares had been particularly vivid this time and she doubted the wisdom of staying in this one-horse town for another day. She debated with herself as she cleaned up and dressed.

She looked at the limp collar of the shirt she'd been wearing since Wednesday night when she'd gotten in her car for the drive. Hard to believe it was Friday morning, almost the weekend. Not that it mattered when she had a couple more weeks before school started.

The shirt smelled a bit rank. *I really need clothes.* Roxy raked her fingers through the damp tangle of her shoulder-length hair. *I need a hairbrush.* Then she bent to examine her freckles in the harsh light of the bathroom. *And I definitely need some makeup.*

There had to be some store equivalent to a Wal-Mart, even in a town this size.

Her stomach rumbled. She patted it. Okay, breakfast first, the bank, and then shopping. She grabbed the twenties she'd accepted from Luke. She looked at them curiously. What was it about him? She'd met all kinds of men; rich successful men and long-haired rebels oozing sensuality. Still, it was the uptight Farmer John who made her want to give herself up to his keeping.

I wonder if he makes love with the same attention to detail as he exercises in his job? A little quiver went through her at the thought.

Roxy pulled a lock of hair up to her cheek. *I hope he didn't get the impression that my offer for him to come into my motel room was payback for his assistance. I feel humiliated enough as it is.* She rubbed the curl against her face. *It doesn't matter. We won't see each other again.* With a sigh, she pushed her hair back off of her face.

Shoving the twenties back into her pocket, she picked up the key to the room. The large ring had a plastic tag in the shape of a cactus with the number fourteen in bright orange. It reminded her of the creative hall passes at the high school.

One of her students had given her a Porsche hall pass he'd made in shop. He'd even painted the eight-inch wooden car the brightest yellow he could find. All the kids admired her car, but at a respectful distance. The tough kids she mentored took care of their own, and that included her. She smiled at the thought of her students. She missed them. They gave her life meaning.

From Luke's car tour of the main street, she remembered, roughly, the location of The Golden Pan. Looking in the windows of the shops along the way she thought the Western Round-Up would do for jeans, shorts and shirts. The drugstore across the street would probably carry toiletries.

It was already getting hot so she entered the air-conditioned lobby with a sigh of relief. Various animal trophies littered the walls. A sign propped up beside the register advertised an opening for a waitress. Roxy noted it absently as she sought out a table. Several cups of coffee and a stack of pancakes quickly followed.

Sometime during her meal she decided being alone would allow her too much time to think, although going home right now wasn't the best option. She felt cowardly, her flight from Dallas proof she wasn't strong enough to face her old drinking crowd. *Maybe I'm fooling myself. Maybe I can't fight this fight. If bad times come around I'll just fold.*

But a bad time had come around and she'd reached for her keys rather than a drink.

It was progress.

Pitiful. But progress.

Idly she watched the pregnant waitress trying to serve all the tables around her. Roxy needed something to pass the time until she was ready to go home, something with long, exhausting hours. Right there, having made yet another impulsive decision she would probably regret, Roxy got the waitress's attention.

ROXY BALANCED the heavy tray full of home-style dinners. As she prepared to put the meat loaf special in front of a customer, the rancher gestured toward the catsup bottle.

"I'd like some catsup, please. The bottle on the table's almost empty."

"Sure. Be with you in just a moment." Roxy finished

handing out plates, asked if the customers needed anything else and then moved to check on her next table.

Roxy had been hired on the spot and had an apron strapped on her faster than you could say "soup of the day." Lisa, the pregnant waitress, had practically kissed her when she'd asked about the opening for a job, even though she made it clear she wouldn't be staying long. Lisa had been even more excited when she'd found out Roxy had experience. It was no big deal. In the years she'd been openly drinking, she'd avoided her dad and thrown his money back in his face. She'd survived by becoming proficient at all kinds of jobs.

A customer with two children was trying to get her attention. "Yes, may I help you?" Roxy asked as she approached the table.

While one child drew on a napkin, the other was yelling. "I need two Dr. Peppers, and a Diet Coke," said the harried mother, "and another pen if you can spare it."

Roxy handed the woman her extra pen. *I'm glad I teach high school.*

She went on to the next table to jot down more drink orders. Suddenly Roxy found herself nodding absently at a customer, having no idea what he'd just ordered. Sheriff Luke Hermann had just walked into the diner with a perfect, petite blonde. He and the blonde settled in a booth beside the lady with the kids.

Roxy gritted her teeth and plastered on a smile. She pretended to finish the order and then she sauntered up to the table where Luke was seated.

Luke dwarfed the little gal. She was slight enough to

look childlike beside him. Her hair was true blond without a hint of red or curl.

There was no way that little Barbie doll had a temper. *I'll bet she doesn't know how to stand up to the man.* She probably just said "Yes, Luke" and "No, Luke" and "Whatever you want, Luke." Roxy ground her teeth.

"Yes, Luke" and "No, Luke" were the last things she wanted to say to him. Although he'd been honest with Roxy, she was stunned at how much it hurt to see them together.

His very surprised reaction to her presence was almost a balm to her ego, so she forged ahead. Best to get this over with—she was sure to run into him as long as she stayed in town. The long arm of the law and all that. "Hello, Luke. You ready to order a drink?" Luckily the drinks in this restaurant were all nonalcoholic.

"Hello, Miss Adams," he stuttered. "How are you feelin'?"

"I'm fine." Roxy's smile went even wider. He looked like a little boy with a handful of forbidden cookies.

"What are you doing here?" He rushed on. "Didn't you get the wire?"

"I got the wire, but I had some time on my hands and Lisa needed help. I dropped the twenties at the police station. Thanks for the loan."

The blonde's head went back and forth between them like a tennis ball. "Luke, care to introduce us?" she asked impatiently.

Maybe she wasn't as blond as she appeared.

Luke gestured toward Roxy. "Carla Rae Sweeny, this

is Roxanne Adams. She had a medical problem yesterday morning and I drove her over to the clinic."

Carla gave Roxy a smile which didn't meet her shrewd eyes. "He's always rescuing strays, aren't you, darling?" She put a possessive hand on Luke's arm.

Roxy noticed Carla's long beautiful nails were painted a nice pale pink. Insipid. Still, if this was what he wanted... "I guess you're the fiancée?"

There was a sudden silence all around them. Carla sat as if stunned. Roxy wondered why. The girl had staked her claim, so why did she look as if her world had just tilted.

"Fiancée?" Carla echoed.

All the stereotypes about blondes must refer specifically to Carla. What part of "fiancée" didn't she get?

Luke looked like he'd just swallowed the meat loaf special whole. His face was as red as catsup.

Finally Roxy got it.

Had Luke used a phony engagement as an excuse not to stay with her last night? Had she just announced a nonexistent engagement in front of a good portion of his town? Had she put her size nine shoe directly into her big mouth?

Carla did have a brain. Roxy had to give her that much credit. And it was clicking away right now. She wasn't likely to let this golden opportunity slip out of her claws.

Roxy watched the wave of gossip ripple through the restaurant. She caught a very ugly look from Luke and suddenly thought of the catsup the rancher had requested. She fled toward the kitchen.

The hallway to the kitchen was quiet. She leaned to peek in to the kitchen; apparently the cook and his assistant had sneaked out for a cigarette break. Roxy took her time looking on the lower shelves for the bottle of catsup. She needed to regain her equilibrium. The cop who acted like a Boy Scout had lied about being engaged. What did that mean? Was it a compliment to her womanly attributes or just a convenient excuse?

"Why the hell did you call Carla my fiancée?"

Roxy came up from under the shelf so fast she whacked the top of her head. Surprise had her stuttering, "Luke, you scared me."

"I scared you? You just coldcocked me. What are you doing here? If I'd have known how much trouble you'd be I would have driven you home to Dallas myself."

Roxy felt such shocked disbelief she almost dropped the bottle of catsup she'd just retrieved from the shelf. "You told me you were engaged. I can't believe you're angry because I repeated what you told me."

"It wasn't for public consumption."

"Luke, it isn't an alcoholic beverage. It's a commitment. That's the nature of an engagement. What's your problem? A Boy Scout like you wouldn't tell a lie unless it was important. I assure you I'd have been fine if you'd just told me you didn't find me attractive, instead of making up an excuse not to come into my motel room."

"It wasn't an excuse. And I'm no Boy Scout." It came out low and hard.

As his civilized veneer cracked wide-open, Roxy realized this wasn't the mild-mannered sheriff from yesterday. His dark eyes blazed with emotions. And it made her knees buckle. She sucked in a breath. All that masculine power made her want what she couldn't have.

"I knew what you were offering but I have a commitment with Carla. I couldn't put that aside despite the way you were looking at me with those big blue eyes."

He looked nothing like a Boy Scout. He looked dangerous and more sexy than ever. She took a step backward. "Well, you can't blame me for simply repeating what you told me."

"I didn't want to go into a long explanation."

"Why not? I would have welcomed the company. I wanted to spend time with you." *Making love to you. Touching you. Would it have been like this? Full of fury? A wild ride? Or would it have been tender and unbearably sweet?*

"It wouldn't have stayed innocent." His words echoed her thoughts. "When you rubbed your leg against me in the clinic I wanted you. I wanted those long lethal legs wrapped around me. I knew if I went into your room I wouldn't leave without tasting you, without having you."

She blushed with pleasure. He sure knew how to take the sting out of his rejection.

Lethal. She liked the sound of that. "So that's why you didn't come in? Why you lied?"

"As you so often remind me, I have a position of authority in this town and a commitment to Carla, even if it isn't formal."

She felt deflated. She concentrated her gaze on the tray in front of her, unwilling to meet his eyes. "Then why are we even having this conversation?"

"Carla and I have been seeing each other for years."

"I understand and I don't plan to get in the way."

"I thought I understood it, too…until you showed up. Then I couldn't remember why I wanted to be with Carla." He ran a hand through his dark hair and his voice grew low, almost as though he was speaking to himself. "I think maybe we settled on each other. And Carla doesn't deserve to be *settled* for. She deserves better."

Roxy shrugged as if she didn't feel a current coursing through her. "You're right. You both deserve someone who's crazy about you but I'm not the one. Any relationship we had wouldn't be long-term. I'm not staying."

His introspective mood disappeared, replaced by a glower. "I don't care for casual sex."

It wouldn't have been casual on my part. I haven't been with anyone in more than two years. But she didn't say it. Instead she mocked him. "And you say you're not a Boy Scout."

"It isn't wise to taunt me after the trouble you've

caused me. I had no intention of humiliating Carla or hurting her feelings."

Roxy slammed the catsup bottle down on the shelf. The bottle knocked a pepper shaker, which rolled onto its side, spilling some of its contents. The pungent smell filled her senses. "So don't hurt Carla. Just consider this an opportunity to shake up your relationship."

She grabbed the pepper shaker. The pepper looked mild, benign, until you stirred it up. If she'd sensed the passion lying below his tranquil surface she never would have teased him or asked him into her motel room.

He was too dangerous.

"I might owe you for showing me that I'd become complacent, and for saving me from a relationship turned comfortable." He paused.

Roxy straightened up and then looked up into his eyes. Did he really mean it? Did he even know what he wanted? Did she?

"But I don't appreciate your meddling," he continued. "Especially when you did it so publicly."

"Don't worry. I'll be happy to oblige your need for privacy, Sheriff. I'll stay so far out of your business you won't see me at all."

"That's not what I want. I told you... Damn it. I can't believe this." He reached down as if he were going to adjust his gun belt. Roxy's eyes naturally followed his motion. Only tonight he wasn't wearing his uniform. He was wearing jeans that clung to his hips like a second skin.

She hurriedly swallowed and then glanced up at his face. Was he blushing again, or just angry?

"Are you always so damn sassy?"

"Yep," she said boldly, thrusting the tray in front of her as if it offered some protection, though she felt as unsteady as the pepper shaker that had tumbled over on its side.

"It's the red in my hair. And the fact that I always got away with being a brat. My dad just couldn't stand to reprimand me. He'd explain why I couldn't do whatever I'd done or say whatever I'd said, and then he'd give me chocolate. Guess it reinforced the habit."

"If I had a little redheaded girl with freckles I'd probably do the same." Luke's face cracked a bemused grin, as if he could see the little girl she'd been.

In that moment Roxy knew she had to get away from him. It was insane to ache for a man like him. A good man with a soft spot for red hair and freckles. *I'm safe. All I have to do is to tell him my secrets and he'll escort me out of town.* Her secrets would disgust him. He thought the engagement announcement was awkward. What would he think of her last binge?

"Luke, I'm not sticking around. You're not into casual sex. And I saw the possessive way Carla held on to your arm. She wants you. Or is all this just an excuse because you're not ready for the ball and chain?" she said flippantly, hoping he'd see the sense of it, or get angry and go away.

"Obligation." He nodded. "That's exactly what I've

been thinking all day long. When did Carla get to be just an obligation? It's not right for either one of us."

"It's just a phase. You'll feel normal again when I leave town."

He pushed closer to loom over her. "You're leaving soon then? Are you running, or are you pretending you're not interested?"

She couldn't meet his eyes. Instead she fiddled with the catsup bottle. "I'm not interested." *I'm running.*

"You know, Miss Dallas, you've been nothing but trouble from the moment I found you on the side of the road."

His high-handed attitude riled Roxy, and she slid the tray onto the shelf, then took a step separating them. She planted her finger in the center of his wide chest. "Why? Because I'm not willing to stick around while you decide whether or not you're going to break up with your girlfriend? Is your ego so big you can't accept that I'm simply not interested in anything other than taking your dinner order?"

"There's something here that needs exploring and I'm going to do what I have to do."

"I'm not a *thing* that needs exploring." Although she could imagine him exploring her with those big hands. She could picture his tanned skin against her white skin, his rough palms cupping her breasts. Roxy took a deep steadying breath. Best to concentrate on other things. "I don't belong here. I belong in Dallas. You don't do affairs and I don't do small towns without shopping malls. Chemistry, curiosity, call it what you will but it will go away."

Especially when I tell you about my past.

He was leaning very close to her now. She could see how long his eyelashes were and the golden flecks in his brown eyes.

She drew back. "Go away. Goldilocks is waiting for you out there."

"I'm not out there. I'm in here," Carla declared from directly behind Roxy.

Luke stiffened. But he didn't move. Roxy was starting to feel downright claustrophobic. Were *all* the customers going to join them?

"Luke, leave her alone." Carla looked up into Roxy's face. "He has a temper, but he won't hurt you."

You make him sound like a pet, not the most arousing man I've ever met.

Luke put a hand on Carla's shoulder. "Carla, go back to the dining room. I'm just helping Miss Adams find the artificial sugar packets for your iced tea."

Carla laughed.

Roxy wanted to shake her. How dense could the girl be? The man she was almost engaged to had been about to kiss the new waitress. Was she a half-wit as well as a half-pint?

"He's just angry with you, Miss Adams, because you spoiled his surprise."

Roxy looked at the girl, really looked at her. She was no girl. There were small lines on her face and a knowing expression in her eyes. Carla knew the score, but she obviously wanted Luke any way she could get him. "Luke was the one who seemed surprised," Roxy told her.

"We had an understanding. Now it's public. Too bad you won't be in town long enough to come to the wedding."

Luke moved so quietly neither of them heard. He put a hand on Carla's shoulder. "We should speak in private, Carla."

"So you won't be having the meat loaf after all?" Roxy asked innocently.

He gave Roxy a warning look and then steered Carla out toward the dining room.

Roxy took a deep breath. She was praying they'd leave the restaurant altogether, but it seemed like too much to ask.

She jumped when Junior, the cook's assistant, tapped her on the shoulder.

"They just walked out the front door," he told her. He was a very young man with ancient blue eyes. Her instincts told her he was in some kind of pain or trouble.

She smoothed her apron. "That's good. I've got a lot of tables to take care of."

"Lisa got some of them."

She waited for him to elaborate and when he didn't, she smiled. "Junior, you're a man of few words."

"Don't cause him any more trouble."

"Why not?" Roxy wondered what Luke and this boy could have in common. "He's the local law. I would think a kid like you would resent him."

"Do I have a sign on my head that says I'm a bad guy?"

No, but I recognize the signs. "I wasn't thinking you're a bad kid. I just thought all kids resented the local law. I'm sure you got caught skinny-dipping or painting cuss words on the water tower at least once."

"If that's your measure of a bad kid then I was the devil. And the sheriff, he bailed me out. Helped me get into college. Get a life. Take my advice and let him alone." Junior turned without another word and walked back toward the kitchen where the cook was back at work.

She smoothed her apron once more. *He's a hero, even to a skinny kid who used to be in trouble. I don't deserve a man like him. And I never will no matter how long I've been sober.*

It was better that she left him to Carla. Carla was exactly the right kind of woman for a man like Luke. Roxy was the wrong kind. Bad girls and Boy Scouts just didn't go together.

4

"I TOLD YOU TO GO and put your feet up. Your ankles are the size of grapefruits." Roxy shook her head at Lisa. "I can't believe you don't trust me to wipe down the tables by myself. How hard can it be?"

"I trust you. I just hate to abuse you on the first day. You might quit on me."

Roxy smiled. Lisa meant it. She trusted a woman she hadn't known more than a day to lock up the restaurant. It felt really good. "Go. I'm coming back tomorrow. I promise."

Lisa rubbed her back. She was so pregnant she really did look like she was going to pop. "Okay. I'm going. I just wanted to apologize for all the fireworks on your first day. I'm sorry about the misunderstanding with Luke—he's really the nicest guy."

"It wasn't a misunderstanding. He *told* me he was engaged," Roxy insisted. Did the entire town look after the local sheriff like he was a favorite son?

"He's probably embarrassed. He wanted to tell her himself. He probably had the ring all picked out and everything," Lisa told her earnestly. There was a dreamy look in her eyes as if she was envisioning the moment she'd become engaged.

Roxy wondered what it would be like to live a life so romantic, you could still reminisce about love when your ankles were swollen up.

Just then Lisa's tall, gangly husband hurried in the front door looking outright panicked. "Lisa, just give her the key. I want you to go home and put those feet up. Doc says you've got to keep that baby in for at least two more weeks, though I don't know where you're going to put any more of him."

Lisa patted her huge stomach affectionately. "I think I'm having the biggest son on the planet."

Roxy smiled at the way the young lovers looked at one another. It was sweet. She shooed them outside and then shut the front door behind her. She didn't lock it. The streets were deserted. Apparently not even a dog dared to stroll along the street past curfew in Red Wing. Luke would probably deny them their kibble if they misbehaved.

She reached into the pocket of her apron where her tips were stored. She separated out the quarters and walked up to the old-fashioned jukebox in the corner. It was a beauty. The entire front of the jukebox was a golden color, and the lights projected through it were soft and mellow. The little window where you could see the machine load the CDs was tinted green. All evening she'd wanted to look at the selection of old songs, but the crowd in the diner had been thick.

Now she took a leisurely inventory of the selections. It was all country music except for a few Elvis songs. There were some Hank Williams, but for the most part the songs were by newer artists. One of her favorite of the country classics, "Eighteen Wheels and a Dozen Roses," was there.

Roxy had counted over four dollars in quarters, and since she was in no hurry to go back to the Cozy Daze, she fed them all into the jukebox.

Around the jukebox was a little space. Lisa had told her that some nights they'd have a fancy dinner and a dance for one of the local organizations.

Roxy swayed along to the song that was playing. She closed her eyes until she bumped into a chair. "Time to get back to work," she muttered, rubbing her hip.

But first she turned off the overhead lights. She would have to be extra careful with her cleaning, but it was nice to be listening to music in the soft golden light. It was another world out here in Red Wing. A world she would make her own for a short time, until she had to go back home and face her demons.

The wiping, rinsing, wiping rhythm soothed her into a mild trance until she finished. She stretched and then walked into the kitchen to throw the rag into a bucket in the sink to soak overnight. Checking to make sure everything was closed and all the lights were out she walked back into the dining room. And almost screamed.

He was standing in front of the jukebox. He was as tall as Lisa's husband but not youth slender. There was power in every line of his masculine body. He looked dark and dangerous and her instincts told her to run out the kitchen door while she still could. But her feet were firmly planted as she watched Luke turn from the jukebox.

"I put more quarters in. Lisa ordered some of these songs specifically for me." His deep voice washed over her. Right away she could sense a quality in it that was different. Dark. Dangerous.

"She thinks you're wonderful. All she could do tonight was worry about you and Carla."

"She told me you were closing tonight so she could go home and put her feet up. She likes you, too."

"It was the least I could do, considering her condition." *What are you doing here? Are you checking up on me or have you come to taunt me with what I can't have?*

"She said you were cleaning up. I'm glad I caught you. I was hoping you didn't intend to leave right away."

"I was wiping the tables. I'm done now." *And I'm babbling like an idiot. He's thinking Miss Dallas is stupid and I'm wishing he didn't look like a dream come true.*

"I'll bet it was busy tonight. Are you tired?"

"No, I'm fine." Her tone was defensive. "You don't have to look after me. I'm an adult."

He looked her over. "You're surely an adult. But you shouldn't mind me looking out for you."

His appreciative look doesn't mean anything. "Don't look at me like that."

His grin was cocky. "Like what?"

I wish he'd find someone else to take care of. I don't want a nursemaid. I don't even want him as a lover. "Like you admire me. You don't even like me."

"I do. I like you, and I'd like to get to know you better." The air sizzled around them. How did he make such an innocent statement sound seductive?

I'm probably imagining it. Frustration surged through her. "I don't need you to feel sorry for me."

"What I feel for you has no resemblance to pity."

"Why are you here?"

His gaze didn't leave hers. "Maybe I couldn't stay away."

"Why? This isn't your style. You don't do casual sex, remember?"

"What's between us isn't casual."

"There's nothing between us but a little chemistry."

"Then why am I aching to hold you?"

She threw up her hands. "Hormones. Your protective instincts. How should I know? Just pretend none of this ever happened. Go back to Carla."

"I want you. I want to find out who you are inside. Uncover all your secrets."

She held her breath. *It's my secrets that will end this foolish game. If I allow myself to have you it'll be just for tonight.*

As if he could read her mind, he held out his arms. "Come and dance with me."

She shook her head. "We can't do that. What about Carla? What about resisting?"

"I took Carla home and straightened things. I told her that I never really meant to say we were engaged and when I did it didn't feel right. I guess I've been dragging my feet because somewhere inside, I knew she wasn't right for me."

Roxy hid behind a chair. "And the resisting part?"

"That was your idea, not mine."

"I don't fit in here and I won't be staying on."

"I'm not askin' you for anything more than a dance."

"Why?"

"Why what?"

"Why would you want to dance with me?" Roxy asked earnestly. "You've been condescending from the moment we met."

"I want to dance with you because you have the longest legs in Texas."

Boy, the man knew how to give a compliment. She walked around the chair on those very legs, which had lost the ability to resist him.

"This isn't a good idea," she said as she approached him in the romantic glow of the jukebox light. He hovered over her yet again. But this time his arms came around her and she laid her head on his chest as if she were finally coming home. A country croon went from melancholy to incredibly romantic and they swayed to the music.

He led her in a slow two-step. The diner disappeared. There was only the feel of her body against his and the crooning of George Strait around them.

One song led to another and Roxy felt misty at the beauty of these endless moments. She didn't want to unwrap herself from him, even to clear her vision. If she could see clearly then she might lose this fleeting fantasy.

It was his hands stroking her hair that awakened her senses. Strong hands so gentle as they explored the texture of her hair. He petted. He stroked. He caressed. His fingers danced over the back of her neck and she shivered.

She tilted her head up, hoping for his kiss. He obliged her. The world tilted. She clung to him while he tasted her thoroughly.

Then he lowered his head, lower until he buried his face in the side of her neck. He laid kisses in a sweet line toward her aching breasts. It made her knees buckle. He tightened his hold as if he knew her every weakness.

And perhaps he did. For he held her, nuzzling her neck until the tempo of the music changed. While the singer told the sad tale of lovers parted, Luke slid his hands down her back.

The hunger grew. She could feel his breath against her nape. The music changed tempo and so did his breathing. She pressed against him and she could feel his blatant arousal, so she pulled back until he stopped her.

"This really isn't a good idea," she repeated softly against the plane of his chest.

"This is not an idea. It's a fact."

Luke put his hands on her bottom and pulled her against him. Then he stopped moving his feet. He kissed her neck and the hollow of her throat. "Your freckles are like brown sugar. I'll have to connect each and every dot with my tongue."

Roxy shuddered as his tongue moved lower toward the deep vee of her top. "It would take you all night. I must have a hundred freckles."

"What a sweet job," he whispered huskily. "I want to see you. Naked."

She nodded.

"I want to feel you."

She nodded again, feeling weak and hugely powerful at the dangerous desire he was keeping in check.

As if he'd been waiting for her permission he put his hands beneath the hem of her denim skirt. Higher and higher he moved up her legs until he grasped the rounded flesh of her bottom through her panties. He kneaded those globes, pressing her against his heated arousal. She burned. She shuddered. Her legs were almost limp. He supported most of her weight effortlessly, swinging them around to the music, in a dance as old as time, yet new to them.

The next time the music changed he pinned her gently against the wall beside the jukebox. With one hand he held her securely. With the other he possessed her breast through her cotton work shirt and bra. When she gasped he kissed her open mouth. He delved deeply, sharing his glorious heat.

Luke kissed her for a blissful eternity. Then his hands became insistent. He expertly freed her breasts and suckled them. She almost giggled with the sheer joy of his touch. It was like the first time, as if she'd die if she didn't get enough of him.

She reached for the buttons on his shirt. There was a sprinkling of hair on his chest, which she stroked. His skin was so warm.

He pushed her skirt down over her hips, impatiently, pulling at her panties, and yet he stopped to run his hands and mouth over each newly unveiled part of her as if she was irresistible.

"I want you."

"Where?" Roxy whispered urgently.

Luke lifted her, leaving a wrinkled pile of clothing at her feet and then laid her upon a table covered by a red checkered tablecloth. Her legs dangled off of the long edge of the table. It was strange. She didn't know if she should draw her legs up or allow them to dangle. "Luke?" she murmured.

He ran a hand down from her belly button to cup the heat between her legs. Roxy couldn't help but curl her legs up. She groaned.

He explored the slippery folds with excruciating attention to detail, just as she'd suspected he would.

She curled up tighter. "Luke?"

His fingers slipped deeper. Bringing her close to what she craved and then dancing away. "Luke!"

"Shh, honey. I'll take care of you."

She lay in a haze of desire while she heard him covering himself. Protecting her. He was a hero. She shifted, needing him. "Luke! Hurry."

He was at her side. "Are you always so impatient?"

He sounded as if he was smiling. She giggled again at the joy of it.

His kiss was fierce and she reveled in his strength. She felt like a feast as he moved, suckling her breasts, running his tongue from her nipples to her belly button.

Then he moved around to the long end of the table. He stood between her legs, cupping her. She shivered, pushing closer to the edge. She looked into his eyes as he slipped his fingers in and out of her body. His eyes were dark with desire. She pressed closer and felt the tip of his arousal, hot and hard against sensitized flesh.

"Please, Luke."

He positioned her at the very edge of the table. The precarious perch felt dangerous, heady, and then he penetrated her.

Roxy thrust against him, taking everything he had to give. The table rocked. Elvis rocked on the jukebox. The sound pounded through her. He cried out and she echoed those sounds, riding along on a tide of ecstasy as the glorious fury swept her away.

It was several minutes later when she realized she was lying naked in a restaurant, spread out like a meal. She groaned, as fresh heat flowed though her.

I should be mortified.

She would have been, but he stroked her sated body as tenderly now as he had before he'd loved her. She closed her eyes, trusting this stranger who'd awakened the woman she thought she'd lost forever.

5

THE AROMA OF COFFEE filtered through the fog of well-being, cocooning Roxy as the sheets on the bed did. Coffee? Was it a dream? She blinked at the drapes adorned with golden cacti and horned toads. No, she was definitely awake and in the Cozy Daze.

She languidly lifted her head off of the pillow. Luke was standing at the foot of her bed holding two foam cups. *Is he real? Did he stay with me last night after all?*

She vaguely remembered him driving her over in an old truck. He'd even come in for a little while and done a fine job of connecting those freckles he'd been admiring with kisses and nibbles that had driven her out of her mind. Then he'd insisted on leaving. She looked over at the other pillow, and there was no indention. He hadn't stayed, but at least he'd come back this morning.

It was flattering. "Why do you have so many clothes on?" she complained. Then as her thought processes picked up… "How did you get into my room?"

"Millie let me in. We have to talk."

"Millie, the maid who doubles as a gossip queen?" Now Roxy was glad she couldn't see his expression in the dim room. "What could possibly be so earth-shattering that you asked her to let you into my room?

I'm not married, I'm free of STDs and I'm not gay. Anything else could have waited until later."

"You're sassy even before you've had your coffee."

"Yep, and you've come to give me bad news. It's always bad news when the man says, 'We have to talk,' in that tone of voice. Don't you think you could wait to tell me the bad news until I've had a shower? It would be more civilized."

"It's not bad news...necessarily."

As far as she was concerned everything about this situation was bad news. Last night he'd made himself a part of her and now she wondered how long it was before she'd have to let him go. It wasn't going to be easy.

But what choice did she have? Every moment with him had been worth it, like going back to the age of innocence. They'd been so hot for each other, like a couple of teenagers. She shivered.

She was just getting reacquainted with the sensual side of herself. But that would end when Luke realized what he'd got a hold of. Then he'd look at her the way he had that first morning, like she was roadkill, and she'd head out. But she'd leave with some great memories to chase away that bad one where the drunk told her she was a pretty girl... *I know Luke can cleanse me of it. I already feel so good.*

He cocked his head. "What are you thinking?"

I'm thinking about you. "Nothing. I don't think before I've had my coffee."

"Then I'm glad I brought the coffee."

A very unpleasant thought occurred to her. "Are you

engaged again? Because if you are I don't think it's fair to break up with me before breakfast."

"I told you last night. I'm not engaged."

She didn't dwell on it. She'd feel guilty later about whatever she might have done to Luke's relationship with Carla. Although she didn't know why she should bother. Carla would have him hog-tied a few hours after she left town.

Roxy sat up with the sheet pulled up to her collarbone as another thought occurred to her. "Is it my car? Did a little old lady with blue hair run into the back of the Porsche?"

"It's not about your car." He sounded weary, as if he'd been up all night pondering. "We just need to talk." He walked over and set the coffee cups down on a little table.

He was so serious. "So talk."

He turned back toward Roxy and then stared like he wanted to get inside her head.

She put a hand to her hair. It was probably a riotous mess this morning. She ran her tongue over her teeth. "If you don't want to talk right this minute, can I head for the shower?"

"I want to talk."

"So what's holding you back?" she asked with exasperation.

He put his hands down as if to adjust his gun belt, and since he was in civilian clothes, he rested them on his hips.

She pulled the sheet high enough to hide her smile.

That was a cute habit he had and it drew attention to his "gun" which was good-sized and well-loaded. She giggled.

"What's so funny?"

"Whatever you have to say cannot be this difficult."

"I can't think when you're lying there naked."

Her ego got an immediate boost. He really knew how to talk to a girl. "How do you know I'm naked?"

"I tucked you in last night. I know you're naked."

"I didn't want to buy a nightgown at the drugstore. They weren't exactly the height of fashion and it seemed pointless at the time." After she'd gotten the waitressing job, she'd nipped out and bought a few essentials before starting work. Now she thought of her toothbrush but decided against it. The policeman had a problem and she had the solution. "You can take off your clothes and join me. You can show me your *gun*."

"I don't think that's a good idea."

She stretched provocatively, sticking one leg out from under the sheet.

"Stop that."

She slid the other leg out from under the sheet. The material barely covered the hollow of her hipbone on the one side and only a little more on the other. Just a little flick of the sheet and he could see it all. "I'll let you shave them." She rubbed her legs together. "I've got a guy friend who's always begging me to let him shave my legs. He's even offered to pay *me* for the privilege."

He put his hand up to his forehead, as if adjusting his

hat this time. "What a thought. You're one dangerous woman."

"Come and give me a ticket."

"For what? We're not going to start that again, are we?"

She pulled just the tiniest bit and the sheet shifted, baring an inch or so of curling red hair between her legs. "You can give me a ticket for indecent exposure."

He shook his head. "I can't tell you how juvenile you sound." But his gaze was all over her. Then he grabbed a corner of the sheet and pulled it down to her knees. "I want to talk."

"Then stop teasing me, and bring me the coffee." She patted the nightstand. "Set it right here."

"Who is teasing whom? Get dressed and I'll give you the coffee and some orange juice."

"You got me some juice?" How thoughtful of him. And she was going to reward him. Right away. "Bring it here. I'm feeling weak."

"If you don't want there to be a whole lot of gossip you'd better get out of that bed and into your clothes."

"Is that a threat?" This was fun and all of her hormones were racing. She wanted him fiercely. She lowered the sheet from her shoulders toward her breasts. His eyes followed. It was as if he touched each inch she revealed with those deep brown eyes. Only she wanted more. "Come closer."

He didn't take his eyes off of her scantily covered breasts—she knew he should have no trouble seeing her beaded nipples through the thin sheet.

He swallowed. "I'm going to have to take you into protective custody."

"Who will you be protecting me from?"

"Me."

Their eyes met. The air sizzled. *I'm going to go up in smoke, but I'm going to die happy.* In that moment there was the unmistakable sound of the door being unlocked.

Roxy pulled the sheet up to her chin.

"Damn," Luke swore in a low voice.

They both looked toward the door as Carla slipped inside the room.

Roxy looked at Luke. "You should have put out the Do Not Disturb sign. We might have had more privacy."

"I doubt it would have mattered." His voice was dry.

Carla put her hands on her skinny little hips. "You won't be needing the sign. Luke's coming with me. I won't let him throw away his career on a woman like you."

"Don't you knock?" She wasn't surprised Carla was chasing Luke down. Roxy couldn't imagine giving him up. If she'd been a woman good enough for him, she would have used his handcuffs on him until he said "I do."

"Luke, I want you to come home with me," Carla demanded.

"Why would he want to do that?" Roxy asked.

"Because you're not decent," Carla declared dramatically.

"I'm not dressed. There's a difference," Roxy pointed out. It wasn't fair. Carla was dressed in a red, traffic-stopping dress.

Carla turned on her. "Of course you're not dressed. You're already giving it away to get your claws in him."

Roxy looked at her fingernails chewed to the quick. "I'm not the one with the claws."

"If you think Luke's going to fall for you, you're sadly mistaken."

"Carla," Luke interrupted mildly.

"He's not going to fall for any out-of-town, one-night stand. He's got a reputation to uphold. Not that you care, but this sort of thing could ruin his chances of getting reelected."

The one-night stand comment didn't hurt much because Luke had come back this morning and the way he'd watched her gave Roxy the distinct impression he wanted to pick up where they'd left off. But, the reelection thing made her pause. "The sheriff's job is an elected position," Roxy mused to herself.

"That's brilliant. *Now* you realize what you've done."

"I don't think the town will run me out on a rail," Luke said mildly.

"But you don't know," Carla said with obvious sincerity. "You may be willing to put me aside but your career is your whole life."

It hadn't occurred to Roxy that Luke might suffer ramifications from their relationship. He shouldn't give up his career because she wanted to be with him for a couple of days. She didn't deserve him. And he didn't deserve what she'd done to him. "No one knows he came here this morning, so his reputation's safe," Roxy insisted.

Carla looked solemnly at Luke. "The whole town knows your pickup was outside The Golden Pan until really late last night. I got six calls."

"The whole town knows?" Roxy repeated. Now she knew why he hadn't hesitated to come into her room this morning, despite Millie, the gossiping maid.

Luke nodded.

"And you're willing to forgive him for humiliating you in front of the entire town?" Roxy asked Carla.

"I am." She said it like it was "I do."

Roxy looked at Luke. "That should go a long way toward fixing the damage I've done."

"I realize," Carla spoke up quickly, "that Luke and I have been dragging our feet on setting the date. We've obviously got issues to iron out. But I think we've got a good chance at making a lasting commitment. We've got a lot in common, the same goals of having children and making a home. We both love this town." She held her arms up toward Luke as if waiting to embrace him.

"I'm no longer content to settle on a *good* relationship, Carla. Loving the town is not the same as loving each other." Luke looked resolute as he said it.

"We're just going through a rough patch because I didn't understand what you wanted. We can go for counseling. I'll change," Carla insisted.

Roxy flinched. She knew she should get into her car and go home. A man like Luke deserved better than the likes of her. "Actually that's pretty decent of you, Carla."

Carla gulped back what might have been a sob and nodded. "Please just go home. You're a city girl. You wouldn't like it here. The gossip alone is likely to kill a person." She wiped her eyes.

Luke stepped forward as if to comfort Carla. The look of sympathy on his face made Roxy squirm with guilt. *What have I done this time? And I was sober the whole time.*

"Carla, I never meant for you—" Luke stopped as if he didn't know what else to say.

Carla didn't even look at Luke, having obviously gotten on a roll. "Now the entire town knows about you. Josie heard the jukebox and she called her sister, and her sister told Mildred. It wasn't long before I got the call. I can only guess where you seduced Luke in that filthy restaurant." She shuddered.

All sympathy for Carla drained out of Roxy. *I'm going to pull all of her golden hair out by the roots for making our time together sound cheap and ugly.* Roxy clenched her hands.

"Carla." Luke's voice sounded patient but there was a thread of warning. The intense look was back on his face.

Roxy felt a little better although she didn't like him looking at Carla in any way, shape or form.

"Carla, just ignore the gossip," Luke told her.

She hurried over to him and threw herself into his arms. "How can you put your job in jeopardy for someone like her?" she sobbed into his chest.

Luke wrapped his arms around her. "My job isn't an issue right now. Elections are a long time away. People forgive and forget."

Look at them. There was a pain in the vicinity of Roxy's heart at seeing them together. They fit. The good guy and the girl next door.

Carla gestured toward Roxy. "She's a rich snob who thinks this is a joke, seducing the local law official for a thrill while she's stuck in Red Wing. She's using you so she can go back and tell her country club set what she did on vacation."

"Don't judge me." Roxy was getting angry. "I really dislike it when people do that. What Luke and I feel is our business." Carla was actually a nice person, just angry because her life was coming apart. Roxy understood that. But it didn't mean she had to take Carla's insults.

"Go ahead, ruin his life."

"Carla. That's not called for. You might be hurting but there's no need to talk ugly to Roxy. I'm the one you want to be mad at."

"I can't be angry with you. I love you."

Bravo. What a performance. Carla had managed to get all the attention. Well, getting attention used to be Roxy's specialty and she knew just what to do. As Luke looked at her over Carla's head, Roxy let the sheet slip a few inches. Carla didn't have much in the breast department. She looked great as a clothes hanger, but Luke deserved a few curves to hang on to. The sheet slipped lower, baring Roxy's breasts.

Carla turned her head from Luke's chest and her cheeks got as red as her dress. "Stop that. Stop that right now."

Roxy gave her a triumphant smile and then pointed at the door. "*You* came uninvited into *my* room this morning, and then you insulted me. It's not my fault I'm not dressed for company." She let the sheet fall to her waist. She'd never liked being told what to do.

Carla looked like she was going to have a stroke. She pulled away from him. "Luke, this is what you want? This floozy? She has absolutely no shame."

"Why should I feel ashamed? I didn't barge into your room and call you names."

Carla just shook her head. "Luke, you'd better reconsider because you're giving up your whole future and I doubt she'll be worth it."

"Pull the sheet up. Honey, please."

Roxy pulled the sheet up to her chin, but only because he'd been admiring, and asked her nicely. He'd even called her honey. She felt good. Guilty as hell, but good.

Luke patted Carla's shoulder.

Roxy had that pain in her chest again. She thought about letting the sheet slip but decided to trust Luke.

"Mark my words, she's going to drive her Porsche right over your heart on her way out of town. And you're going to end up pumping gas or selling cars."

Roxy folded and unfolded a corner of the sheet. She could just imagine the limited job market in Red Wing.

He threw Roxy an apologetic glance. Then once again

he concentrated on Carla. "Then I'll sell cars. This isn't about Roxy," Luke told Carla.

"Yeah, right. She's just an innocent bystander."

"You might call her a catalyst. Because suddenly I realized I was settling for a comfortable marriage. Because it was expected and because I wanted to stay in this town." He shrugged. "But we both know something's missing."

A catalyst? Roxy didn't know if she liked the sound of that. "I don't think I like being a catalyst." Why couldn't he have said something like irresistible or overwhelming?

"Shut up," Carla told her. "This isn't about you!"

"Don't tell me to shut up," Roxy said with dignity. She let the sheet slip a few inches.

Luke noticed right away.

Carla glowered at her.

Roxy smirked.

"Carla, this is just making matters worse. I think you should go home.

"But Luke..." She pouted prettily. "I've been good to you for years. I love you."

"You might love me, and then you might just love the idea of being a sheriff's wife. We've been over this."

"This is so unfair."

"I'm sorry. It didn't matter to me before because we would have both gotten what we wanted, but now I'm looking for something...different."

Roxy thought she was going to burn up when he

turned his intense look on her. Her hand loosened on the sheet.

"Luke, make her stop that!"

Luke tore his gaze away from Roxy and looked at Carla.

"If you want her, then go ahead and get her out of your system. When you're done using her I'll be waiting for you, Luke. I'll be hurting, but I'll take you back." Carla followed up her dramatic statement with a theatrical march across the room, and then punctuated it with a resounding door slamming.

Roxy felt both relief and chagrin once Carla left. Luke shook his head very gently, as if reassuring Roxy. He was so wonderful. It made Roxy angry. A flush ran down her neck. She was furious at herself for the mistakes she'd made—mistakes that would always come between her and the things she wanted. Luke. She wanted Luke.

And as suddenly as it had come, the anger drained away. Carla was right. She and Luke were not compatible because Roxy couldn't stay in this town and Luke wouldn't leave. She wrapped her arms around herself, the sheet tight over her breasts.

He grinned, almost licking his lips at the sight of her nipples through the thin sheet.

She felt the corresponding tingle in her breasts and deeper. *I just want him for a little while. Just long enough to make more wonderful memories. Is it so much to ask?*

Luke moved toward the end of the bed and put a possessive hand on her ankle.

"Maybe you should listen to Carla."

He shook his head. "I played it safe too long. Carla isn't what I want."

He slowly slid his hand from Roxy's ankle to her sensitive instep.

"What do you think you're doing? Why aren't you worried about your job security?" Her voice was shrill.

He bent over to look into her face. "I'm more worried Carla's convinced you that I think you're a one-night stand. In just a minute I'll tell you what I think of you. Up close and real personal."

Good gosh, he was lethal. "I'd like my coffee and a shower, in that order," she said primly. Though she felt anything but prim.

Luke ran his fingers gently over her calf.

"Millie will be here to clean my room any minute," she warned him.

This time he nodded his agreement. "I want to take you somewhere."

At the words "take you" she almost moaned. He looked at the sheet as if he could see through it, like Superman.

"Okay. Where?" What damage could one more day do?

"It's a surprise." His fingers caressed the underside of her knee. She didn't gasp. Instead she clutched the sheet with all her defenses firmly in place.

"Like a date?"

"Yes, like a date."

"Okay. What should I wear?"

"Something sexy."

"So this is like a date with...sex?"

"Sounds good to me."

Roxy pushed his hand away. "Yeah, promises, promises. You'll change your mind when Carla grabs you right outside the door."

His eyes bored into her. "No way," was all he said.

Then he got up, strode across the room, opened the door and let himself out. She heard him turning the knob from the outside, making sure the lock had engaged.

"Lot of good it will do," she muttered to the empty room. "Boy, am I going to give Millie a piece of my mind when I see her. She'll get no tip from me."

Roxy took a deep breath and pulled the sheet closer. Luke's promise had sounded more like a pledge. He meant to have her, today anyway.

She hugged herself, burning up but still clinging to the security of the sheet. Better remember, he's a dangerous man.

Potentially addictive.

No. I'm not hooked. I can't afford to go there, no matter how strong the temptation.

Resolutely, she leaped out of bed and promptly fell flat on the floor in a tangle of sheets.

6

THE ENTIRE TIME she was showering Roxy was listening for the sound of the door to her motel room, just in case Millie let Luke back into her room again.

So I'm a bit paranoid, she told the Roxy in the mirror with the limp curls hanging all around her shoulders. No one would blame her when she'd just had two uninvited guests in her room before she even had her eyes open.

The phone rang.

Roxy ran out into the room to pick up the receiver. "Hello?"

"Roxy?"

"Hey Mick. You sound awful."

"Your dad gave me enough coffee to kill me. Still, I'm pretty hung over."

"My dad's the best."

"He's okay. I called to say I'm sorry if I laid any of this mess on you. I wasn't thinking. I guess you paid me back by sending your dad after me."

"Come on. Would you rather have woken up on the street this morning? At least this way you can go soak your head in the hot tub and stretch out by the pool."

"I guess."

"Mick, when you see Joey today tell him that I'll be home to visit him, soon."

"I'm not sure what to say to him, Roxy."

"You don't have to say much. Just sit by his bed. He'll understand you're there for him."

"Yeah. This family stuff is great."

"You know they're pretty sure that addiction is hereditary."

"Yeah, I got it from watching my old man get drunk every night," he scoffed, sounding both sad and angry.

"Well, that's part of it, too," she told him patiently. "If your parents drink you're more likely to try it, and when you try to quit, you suddenly realize you've got a serious problem."

"Getting to know you made me realize it didn't have to do with growing up poor. This place is amazing."

"The situation's actually easier to hide when you can afford to send your wife away for months at a time and let the professionals handle your problems."

"I thought you loved your old man."

"I do love him. He made mistakes and he paid for every one of them."

There was a long silence.

"I owe you, Roxy."

"I owed you first. I can never repay you for the help you gave me when my dad and I were at odds. You were my family. You gave me a job and kept me together."

"A job at a bar. I don't think it did you much good."

"I ate regularly." *And I never had to prostitute myself.*

She didn't want to know how low she would have sunk to get a drink. Being too drunk to realize whom she'd gone home with *that* night had been bad enough.

"I saw a picture of your brother hanging on the wall."

"His name was David."

"You never talked about him."

"I can't handle it—the memory of finding him after he committed suicide." Her hands and voice shook, and she had to grab the receiver in both fists.

"I'm sorry. You help Joey and me and this is a fine way for us to repay you."

She sat down on the edge of the bed. "It's okay. I'm okay."

"Don't get into any trouble."

"What kind of trouble am I going to get into out here in the boonies? This is a town where everyone meddles in everyone else's business." *Like Carla, who actually had a point. I'm putting Luke in jeopardy and he doesn't deserve to lose his whole life because of someone like me.*

"I guess scrutiny like that would keep you walkin' a straight line."

"Yeah, the women here just want lots of kids, and they roll up the streets when the sun goes down."

"Sounds like a good place. An old-fashioned place away from temptation."

"You going to be all right?" she asked.

"Yeah."

"Good."

"'Bye."

She put down the receiver, relieved that Mick sounded okay. She stood up and then went back into the bathroom and picked up her hairbrush. The detangling of her curls was less painful than her thoughts.

Poor me...poor Mick. Addiction was such a predictable cycle. There had been years when she'd held down a full load of college classes and no one had any idea she was drinking again. Just enough to make it through the day, she'd told herself, and for a long time it had worked. Then David had died. Suddenly she'd needed a lot more alcohol to make it through the days.

Addiction meant you needed it.

The woman in the mirror still needed a drink. That was part of it. Since November 19, the day she'd quit drinking, she'd needed alcohol. So she looked to God to help her get through one day at a time, and she tried to make amends for her past mistakes where she could.

And now there was Luke.

How much could one more day cost him? He seemed sure the town will forgive and forget. *And in a day or two I'm outta here as fast as my Porsche will go.*

The woman in the mirror looked back at her with ageless eyes. As long as she remembered this was temporary. She couldn't have him. He was too pure for her. She'd be better off with someone like Mick who knew all about where she'd been, not some fresh-faced Farmer John who still knew how to blush.

And then there was Carla.

He'd made it pretty clear he didn't want Carla.

But Roxy hadn't told him anything about her past.

And Carla had told him that she'd forgive him. She'd be all over him once Roxy left town.

A niggling pain had her rubbing the skin over her heart. *One day. I'll just enjoy him for one more day. All of him. I can't get addicted to him in just one day.*

She fluffed her hair. She looked like hell, with her freckles standing out in stark relief. Too bad. She hadn't bought the thick tan base they carried in town, not with her light skin, and anyway, he'd seen her worse. He was crazy enough to like freckles. She slanted a golden color on her lips and some taupe shadow on her eyelids. She did her lashes. When she was finished she looked reasonably presentable.

She smoothed the front pockets of her shorts. What was she supposed to wear? Where were they going?

She stepped out of the still-steamy bathroom into a silent room. She looked around, not sure what her next move should be. This dating stuff was pretty new to her. The message light was blinking on the phone. She must not have heard it over the blow-dryer.

She tried to check her excitement, but she knew she was smiling as she walked around the bed and then picked up the receiver, hoping it was Luke.

This is crazy. I feel like a stupid yo-yo.

Luke's message made her smile wider. She picked up the little purse she'd bought yesterday and then grabbed her room key. Roxy had no intention of keeping him waiting any longer. Apparently they were going out to breakfast.

He was sitting in a pickup truck outside, in the far

corner of the parking lot where a scrawny tree shaded the cab of the truck. It was already hot. Roxy was glad she hadn't bothered with much makeup; she felt like she was melting. He got out of the truck as she approached.

"Are you feeling okay?" he asked her looking intensely into her face.

"I'm fine," she chirped. *Don't ask me. I'm barely hanging on to my composure. I feel crazy happy when I'm with you, devastated when I think about everything else. Distract me. Seduce me.*

She looked him up and down. "I didn't have a lot of thinkin' in mind. I'm on vacation. I want to be romanced by the sexy guy who came into my motel room."

"Yeah, this is a hot vacation spot. Jump in and I'll show you all the scenic wonders of Red Wing."

"All of them?" she purred.

Luke grimaced as his body immediately responded. He was easy where she was concerned. He just wanted her. All of her. He held open the passenger side door to the pickup and for all her bold talk, she hesitated like he was asking for a commitment she couldn't make.

It was like he was sixteen again and she was the head cheerleader he desperately wanted to put his hands on. It had taken him about three years to get over that girl. *What am I setting myself up for this time?*

She turned away from the door to face him. "I can tell you're dying to ask me a bunch of questions. I'll only go to breakfast if you promise to feed me right away. No questions. Just food and maybe some...dessert."

Well, she sure moved faster than the cheerleader. He nodded. "In that order?"

She grinned. She was beautiful this morning but there was something else. Something that had bothered him from the beginning. She was hurting and it was more than just the diabetes. It made him itchy to know her secrets.

He couldn't help but admire those lush legs as she crawled into the pickup. She just about had his tongue hanging out of his mouth as her shorts rode up to the top of her thighs. The way he felt, they might not make it to the house. He'd just throw her down on the seat and do her until they turned into a pile of sweat.

The pickup started for home. It was a good thing he had to look at the road because he was as randy as a bull. She was trouble all right. He was starting to believe she was the kind of trouble you didn't get over.

AS THEY LEFT ALL SIGNS of civilization behind, Roxy gave in to her curiosity and the flutter of hunger in her stomach. A hunger to know him. "May I ask where we're going?"

"I want to cook you breakfast."

Roxy's traitorous body immediately escalated the flutter. What was it about a rough man in an old truck? *Whoa, girl. Don't let him get you into bed for the price of a few eggs. No, hold out for toast and bacon.*

She turned away from him to watch the uniform

landscape. It was better if she didn't say anything. She was afraid of what might come out of her mouth if she tried to speak with her hormones working overtime.

By the time they pulled up to an old farmhouse Roxy had shored up her defenses. She noticed his police car was parked here at his house. She didn't have time to notice much else because suddenly two huge dogs were sticking their noses right on her window, steaming it up.

She paused, having no intention of opening her door in the face of those giant teeth. Unfortunately Luke came around and opened the door before she could tell him the dogs were just a tad intimidating. He took her hand and practically pulled her out of the cab.

The dogs sniffed her politely. There was no jumping or snapping. It was bad enough that their noses reached her waist. "What kind of dogs are these? They're the size of miniature horses."

"They're wolfhounds. I inherited them from a guy who had to go away for a while. They're very well trained and they won't jump on you."

"That's good because you'd have to pick my butt up out of the dirt if one of them so much as laid a paw on me. They're huge."

"Are you afraid of dogs?"

"I don't know. I've never had a dog." There'd been times when she couldn't keep an apartment for more than a few months before she drank up the rent money. When she did have a place she couldn't have kept a plant alive unless it liked tequila.

"I forgot. Rich kids probably have dogs in a kennel so they never see them."

"This rich kid had a barn with a horse, but no dogs. Sorry to disappoint you."

He led her toward the farmhouse. "You like horses?"

She nodded. "I love horses."

"I ride sometimes along the dry riverbed with a friend of mine. After a storm you can find all kinds of things the water's dredged up. I give Indian relics and fossils to the museum in Big Spring." He glanced at her. "What kind of horses does a rich girl ride?"

"Felix."

"A felix?"

He stepped up on the porch. The white paint was peeling in some places. There was no porch swing.

Then he just reached out and opened the door.

Roxy could feel her jaw drop open. "Why don't you lock your door? Do the dogs keep people away?"

He shrugged. "I guess they would, but out here there's no one to lock the doors against. No one comes out here unless they live out here."

Roxy turned to look out at the land around the house. It was flat and covered with tall brown grass. It stretched to the horizon. The azure sky was full of puffy white clouds.

"Those clouds will burn off before midday. The sky will be pure, unrelenting blue." Suddenly he was right behind her. His breath was warm on her neck. "It's got its own beauty if you look hard enough."

She flushed. "I know. The sunsets are spectacular."

He touched her hair. "What kind of a horse is a felix?"

She stood still because she didn't want to distract him from stroking her hair. It felt wonderful. "It's not a kind of horse. It's the name of *my* horse."

"It's nice to know you had just a regular horse. Now I won't be so intimidated by your upbringing."

Roxy was glad he couldn't see her face. Felix was now permanently out to stud, but in his day he'd been a very successful racehorse. She'd loved riding him. Even now it still felt as if she were flying when she rode him around the track. "When I was little I wanted to be a famous jockey," she confided.

He raised the hair off of her neck and blew on the overheated skin. Roxy shivered.

"I'll bet you gave Felix quite a workout while you pretended he was a racehorse."

Roxy couldn't suppress a small chuckle. "You got that right. I was burning up the track."

His finger strayed down her neck.

She shied away. "Don't. I'm sweating."

"I know. I like it."

"You like sweat and freckles? You're crazy."

Thankfully he pulled away before she collapsed into a little pile of mush at his feet, begging him to make love to her.

"Come inside and tell my why you didn't become a famous jockey." He gestured toward the cool air coming out of his front door.

"Besides the fact that I'm ten inches too tall? *Ahh,* air-conditioning," she raved as she entered his cozy house.

"Of course. All the comforts of the civilized world at a slower pace."

She looked around curiously. It was definitely not him. The furniture wasn't Western and rugged. Instead the couch was covered in a material worn almost to gray with huge blue and green roses.

"I know it's not manly, but it was my mother's. My sister didn't want it. She left town before the ink was dry on her graduation papers. I didn't have the heart to throw it away, and it's all broken in. You can put your dirty feet on it and I won't mind."

He set down his sunglasses on a beautiful kitchen table with a granite top. "Just make yourself at home."

"What?" she asked absently as she ran her hand over the pattern on the table. Every color of red, orange, and yellow snaked through the granite. There were even subtle black and gold flecks. It looked like a slice of the Grand Canyon. "This is beautiful."

"I got the table after the one I had lost a leg. I found it in the Hill Country. It reminds me of a dry riverbed."

A dry riverbed? Was he being poetic? "It's incredible."

He ducked his head as if he'd bought it on impulse and was embarrassed to admit it.

"It was damn inconvenient when I had to drive back out there with a trailer to pick it up."

She shouldn't allow herself to moon over a man who bought a beautiful table and matched it with his mother's ancient chairs. But the situation was spinning out of her control. The more she found out about Luke the more she wanted him.

She *would* leave though. Right after they fooled around again. This heat between them didn't have anything to do with affection...or love. He just turned her on. Didn't he? She wasn't actually coming to need him.

A distraction was required. "I think the table could use some new chairs. I know of a place where you could buy some which would look wonderful with this table."

He looked honestly confused. "The chairs are still in pretty good shape. I replaced the nails myself."

"I see." And she did. Men were the same all over.

Roxy's stomach rumbled. An excellent distraction. Except Luke's grin made her stomach roll and did something hot and tingly to the rest of her.

"I guess your stomach's reminding me of my promise to give you breakfast."

"That's it," she said. Pretending to herself that she intended to resist this chemistry, Roxy quickly sat in one of the awful chairs to hide the fact that her knees were feeling weak. "What have you got to eat? Doughnuts?"

He looked wounded. "I'll have you know I can cook."

She traced the winding pattern in the granite. "What exactly can you cook?"

"Eggs, bacon, toast and meat loaf."

"We're having meat loaf for breakfast?"

"No, but I can cook it," he told her proudly.

"Together we could probably come up with an entire meal," Roxy told him.

"What can you cook?" he asked.

He was probably waiting to compare her with Carla, the superwoman. Well, he'd be disappointed. It would only make it more clear how unsuited they were to each other. "Dessert. I can only cook dessert."

"How did that happen?"

"My mother was in and out of hospitals when I was young. I barely remember her. We have a terrific cook and I was supposed to stick my head in the kitchen and learn to cook. But I was only interested in cooking desserts. You name anything chocolate and I can cook it."

"Brownies? From scratch? I can make them from one of those boxes."

"I can do brownies," she confirmed with a smile. "All kinds of brownies and even chocolate soufflé. My brother used to try to make it fall flat by dancing around the kitchen, but it usually turned out just fine." Roxy smiled at this memory of her brother. She'd forgotten him dancing in front of the ovens. Now that she thought about it, she'd blocked out all of the good things along with the bad.

"Didn't your brother like soufflé?"

"He did, but I was the one who'd learned to make it and so I refused to share. I also had the staff wrapped around my little finger, mostly because they feared my terrible tantrums. I always got what I wanted.

"Unfortunately for him, my brother was too proud to beg and too dignified to resort to a tantrum."

Luke reached up into a cupboard and grabbed a pan. "I think I like your brother."

Roxy shook her head. No, he wouldn't. What would he say if he knew that David overdosed on Ecstasy? If he didn't turn from her with disgust, he would when she told him that she was once a drunk. A drunk every bit as ugly as a wino on the street.

He caught her distress. "Is it hard talking about your brother? Did something happen to him?"

Roxy nodded. "I don't want to go into it. Okay?"

He waved the pan in the air. "Then you should make yourself useful and get the eggs. I could use the help of a woman who can make a soufflé."

As she collected the ingredients from his surprisingly well-stocked refrigerator, she collected her emotions. It was best to keep the conversation going. It kept both the memories—and the desire—at bay.

He was devastating when he was domestic. "Where's your sister living now?" she asked. It seemed like a safe topic.

"She's in Houston. She's married and has a daughter." He cracked an egg over the pan with little regard for the pieces of shell going in with the eggs.

Roxy washed her hands and then used a spoon to fish the eggshells out of the pan. She looked up to find herself within kissing distance and pulled away. His face was shadowed by beard stubble and she knew it was because he hadn't had much time to sleep or shave since last night.

She said the first thing that came to mind. "Do you always barge into women's motel rooms in the morning? Or am I special?"

"You're special."

She had no idea what to say next. She made sure her mouth was firmly closed while he put the pan over the gas flame on the stove.

"Do you work?" he asked, watching the pan as if her answer didn't matter much to him.

"Would you mind if I was just a lazy slug who lived off of my father's money?"

"I don't know. I guess I'd like to indulge my hobbies if I didn't have to make a living."

"What hobbies?"

"Archeology, of a sorts. I'd like to dig out some spots where we've found Indian artifacts. I think there could be a big find in this area."

"That's neat."

He turned the bacon. "You haven't told me if you indulge a hobby or lie around the pool like a slug." His eyes brushed the length of her body. "You must have a personal trainer. You have fantastic legs."

She could feel herself blushing, all the way down to the legs he'd mentioned. His sweet compliments and incredibly sexy body had her tongue practically hanging out of her mouth. If she didn't say something, quick, she'd insist that he show her to the bedroom even before they ate the bacon and eggs.

"Well, I did indulge a hobby for a long time. I liked college and went to school for quite a few years." *Then I stopped being able to control my drinking, got kicked out of my father's house, and lived from hand to mouth until I went back to rehab.*

"I went to college in Houston."

"You did? I can't imagine you'd like Houston."

He shrugged. "My parents thought we should see what was out there. I majored in law enforcement and took some classes in archeology. What was your major?"

"I majored in math." *I actually majored in avoiding getting caught drinking. I majored in trying to control something that was controlling me instead.* "I thought numbers were straightforward. Tidy."

He finished the bacon and poured the eggs into the pan. "Did you ever finish your degree?"

"Eventually." *After being in and out of rehab, after drinking myself into a hole so deep I couldn't see my way out of it.* "Where are the plates?"

"In the cupboard over there." He pointed with a spatula. "Do you do anything with your degree?"

"This and that." She set the table and resisted the urge to look at him. Let him think they were very different because it was the truth.

"I'll bet you do charity work, drives for children, hospital galas, that sort of thing. Your father must be very proud of you."

Roxy looked up in disbelief. "What? You think I'm some sort of debutante?" This was even worse than if he knew what she really did for a living.

He approached the table with a plate in each hand.

His gaze was as hot as the food. "I would love to see you in a little black evening dress."

"I'm a high school math teacher," she blurted out. "I never go to school in a little black dress."

He set the food down on the table and looked at her face for a moment. He seemed as serious as he'd been when he'd first tapped on her car window. Was it really only two days ago?

"You're full of contradictions. Every time I think I have you pegged, you surprise me."

She shrugged. "Sorry." His instincts were probably right on. *What would you think if you knew that the only job I could get was at the poorest, most understaffed school in the Dallas area?* While her personal credentials were not great, her academic credentials were excellent. And the endowment from her father had helped. "I've been teaching for two years. I love it."

He waited until she'd seated herself before he sat down. "Don't be sorry. I like the unexpected. In my profession you tend to get jaded. It's nice to be surprised." He nodded at the food. "Do you trust me?"

She looked down at her plate. The food looked good. But it was a loaded question. She took a sip of coffee. "I guess I do."

"Then eat. I've got the whole day off. Maybe we'll take the horses out. There's a saltwater pond nearby and it's a great place to cool off."

Naked? was the question which came to her one-track, naughty mind.

"Saltwater?"

"This part of the continent used to be an ocean. The salt is still in the soil and so there are places where the water coming up from underground is close to ocean salinity."

"That's weird."

"It's water and we don't have enough to be picky."

She stuffed a forkful of scrambled eggs into her mouth and made the mistake of looking at him. He wasn't eating. He was watching her. There was desire in his eyes. She wondered if they'd even make it to the pond.

She had a sudden image of herself lying on this table. The granite cooling her skin, Luke heating her up.

She practically choked on the eggs.

The phone rang. It took him a minute, then he blinked and reached for the sleek black phone.

"Yeah?" He listened for a moment. "What?"

He looked down at his watch.

"It'll take me twenty minutes and that's with the lights. Hold tight." Then he hung up.

"You have an emergency?" Roxy sagged in her seat. She felt like the call had let all the air out of her and saved her at the same time. "You have to go?"

He was already up. He pulled a set of keys from his jeans. "These are the keys to the truck. Just go back into town. I'll catch up with you later."

She nodded. Then she stood up, unsure how to help him.

"Can you get back to town okay?"

"There were only two turns," she told him. "One at

the highway to the right, and then left at that abandoned farmhouse."

"Good. You're very good." He came over and pulled her into his arms. His kiss was hot and insistent, even though he touched nothing but her mouth.

"Hold that thought," he told her and then he was gone.

Roxy sank back down into the ugly chair. There was no strength in her legs.

7

ROXY DROVE HIS TRUCK back to the motel with no mishaps. After checking her sugar levels, she grabbed her bathing suit. She swam laps to cool her frustration. It took a long time. Luke had a scintillating effect on her. Afterward she huddled under an umbrella, because she didn't tan. Her freckles just got closer together.

Where was he? How long did an emergency take? Why hadn't he told her what it was? Didn't he trust her? Hot and bothered by more than the rising temperature, she headed indoors. It was so hot the cement seemed to be puddling beneath her feet.

A quick rinse, a comb through her hair, and then she was ready to get some lunch. The air conditioner in the pickup didn't start blowing out cool air until she'd arrived at the restaurant. *It's time to pick up the Porsche.*

Being in his pickup felt good. As if she had a tie to him. *You've got it bad, girl.* She should get in her car and drive to Colorado where it wasn't so hot. Vail was wonderful this time of year.

She grabbed the handle of the door to The Golden Pan, and the metal seared her. She rubbed her fingers on her shorts. *See what it's like here?* she told herself. All they had was old trucks with bad air-conditioning and you couldn't even get into the restaurant to cool off and get something to eat.

She should go somewhere—Italy, Paris, or diving in the Bahamas. Anything would be better than falling for someone like Farmer John in Hades.

But there was no one like Luke in Italy or the Bahamas. She'd already checked.

She finally managed to open the door and entered the nice cool restaurant. It was full of activity. Not what Roxy would have expected for a Saturday afternoon in an otherwise empty town. She grabbed Lisa by the arm. "Hey, what's up?"

Lisa's face was moist despite the air-conditioning. "It's crazy around here."

"Aren't you supposed to be taking it easy?"

"We're making sack lunches for the volunteers. The fire's almost under control but they can't leave yet. It'll probably be evening before they can be sure they've gotten all the hot spots."

"What fire?"

"Where have *you* been? There was an accident this morning. A truck hauling flammable material turned over on the edge of the road. They pulled the driver out in time but the truck exploded, setting the grass on fire. It swept through Walter Green's place and all the volunteers were called up."

"Luke got called away from breakfast..." *I guess I know what he's been doing all morning while I've been feeling sorry for myself.*

Lisa's eyebrows rose, then she said, "Yeah, he's always the first to know. I expect they called the volunteers right after they called him. I'm sorry if it inconvenienced you?" It was definitely a question.

Roxy shook her head hastily. "No, it was all right."

"This time of year when they put a fire call nearly everyone goes. When it's this hot and dry it doesn't take long for a fire to get out of control."

"Of course. I hope everyone's okay."

"We haven't heard if there were any injuries. Are you worried about Luke?"

"Of course not," Roxy insisted. She hadn't thought to hold her tongue. It seemed pointless when Millie had been letting people in her motel room all morning. "I'm not worried about anything."

Lisa looked concerned. "Roxy, I know you mean well, but Luke and Carla are engaged. I don't want to see you get hurt."

"It's okay. I have no illusions about Luke. He and Carla came to my motel room this morning to...ask me if I needed anything. I'm pretty clear on how they feel about each other."

"How nice of them to look out for you. How do you like Carla? I just love Carla," Lisa went on as if afraid of how Roxy might respond. "She was the only one in town willing to go and train up as a special education teacher. We've got three of those special kids—one's my cousin, you know, and without Carla he and my aunt would be lost."

Roxy's smile felt fixed on her face. "She's special all right." How much worse could it get? *Just my luck to try to compete with a local heroine. And I usually like anyone with enough gumption to work with kids....*

As if she just remembered she was working, Lisa grabbed hold of Roxy's arm and dragged her along toward the kitchen. "I hope the two of you get to be real good friends."

"Yeah." Roxy looked around for a way to escape. "Is there anything I can do to help out?"

The phone rang in the lobby, signaling Roxy's escape from Lisa.

Lisa nodded distractedly. "You can help make the sandwiches. Junior will show you how to do it. Cook's out fighting the fire."

She hurried away to the phone.

Roxy took a deep breath. She hadn't lied to Lisa, just misled her a bit. *What was I supposed to say?* she asked herself. *Luke and I made love on one of the tables last night and it was the most beautiful thing that's ever happened to me. I can't believe you're the only one in town who doesn't already know. And, by the way, I think Carla's history.*

That would only lead to more uncomfortable questions. Then Lisa would definitely ask her intentions toward Luke. And she'd say that Luke was a big boy who could take care of himself. If he wanted to be with her he had to understand it was just temporary. He couldn't think they would have any sort of life together. He might not know about her past but he knew where she was from. They were Miss Dallas and Farmer John. Nothing long-term would ever work between us. She wasn't good enough for him and never would be.

Roxy rubbed her eyes and went to find Junior. Time to stop feeling sorry for herself and do something useful.

In the kitchen Junior was humming a country tune while he piled roast beef on slices of bread. He looked up from his task without enthusiasm as Roxy approached. "I thought you'd go home today after that scene with Carla."

Which one? "I don't scare easily."

"Just your second day in town and you've already stirred things up. Even when I was in trouble, I never caused such a ruckus in such a short amount of time."

"I don't know what you're talking about. I just thought I'd help out." Roxy tapped her foot on the ground. He didn't intimidate her.

"Don't need no help."

Roxy put her hands on her hips. She dealt with young people with attitude all day long. Junior acted exactly like the kids who came into her class and challenged her authority or ignored it. She knew how to handle him.

"Lisa looks frazzled. She sent me in here to help you out. But if you don't need any help I'll go and lie out by the pool. Why should I care if she has the baby early?" She spun on her heel as if she would really leave.

For a moment she thought she'd overplayed her hand. He let her get several steps away before his voice stopped her.

"I guess I could use a hand. If I can finish these sandwiches then Lisa can take a break while I run them out to the volunteers."

Roxy spun around during his speech. It wasn't exactly an apology but she'd take it. "Sounds like a good idea."

She watched as he finished the sandwich. All the ingredients were laid out on the counter. He wrapped a sandwich and stuck it in a large bag. Then he handed her a knife.

She held it in front of her like a weapon, assuming a samurai pose. "Should I assemble or cut the meat?"

"I'll cut. You assemble."

She bent her head over the bread to hide her smile at his taciturn answer. *I must be losing my charm.* Fortunately Luke didn't seem to think so.

She reached for an apron and gloves.

They worked in silence for about twenty minutes. The bag was bulging when Junior stopped cutting and then put the remaining meat in the huge walk-in cooler.

Roxy looked at the cooler with longing. "I bet it feels wonderful in there."

He didn't make eye contact but his body language seemed more relaxed. "I was really startled the first time I went in there. The door closed behind me and I didn't know if I was locked in. I thought I was going to die."

Roxy smiled encouragingly. It was the longest speech she'd heard out of him. "I'm a bit claustrophobic. I don't think I'd like to be in there after all."

"How can you drive such a little car if you're claustrophobic?"

"You've seen the Porsche?"

Get FREE BOOKS and a FREE GIFT when you play the...

Just scratch off the gold box with a coin. Then check below to see the gifts you get!

YES! I have scratched off the gold Box. Please send me my **2 FREE BOOKS** and **gift for which I qualify.** I understand that I am under no obligation to purchase any books as explained on the back of this card.

342 HDL DZ9Z 142 HDL D2AG

FIRST NAME LAST NAME

ADDRESS

APT.# CITY

STATE/PROV. ZIP/POSTAL CODE

(H-T-07/04)

7	7	7	Worth TWO FREE BOOKS plus a BONUS Mystery Gift!
cherries	cherries	cherries	Worth TWO FREE BOOKS!
bell	bell	clover	TRY AGAIN!

www.eHarlequin.com

Offer limited to one per household and not valid to current Harlequin Temptation® subscribers. All orders subject to approval.

▼ DETACH AND MAIL CARD TODAY! ▼

"All the kids have been driving by the gas station. I think Larry's done more business in sodas and gas in the last few days than he usually does all month."

Roxy laughed. "Good for him."

"Why haven't you picked up your car?"

"I haven't needed it."

He ducked his head. "I saw Luke's truck here last night. I guess he gave you a ride."

Roxy blushed. How to handle this? "Luke came by to see if I was feeling okay. I was sick when he found me on the side of the road."

"And you reward him by causing him to break up with his girlfriend?"

Roxy flinched. Was the whole town set on protecting the sheriff? "I don't think it's any of your business."

"I watched for a long time. He played all his favorite songs on the jukebox."

"What were you doing watching the restaurant? Don't you have a home to go to?"

"I don't sleep much. Do you mean to stay on? Or are you taking off soon?"

Roxy smoothed the front of her apron. "I have to go back soon."

He nodded. "You don't fit in here."

"I don't think you're being fair. I wonder why you feel you have to protect Luke. I imagine he can take care of himself."

"I owe him."

"For what?" she asked.

"Nothin'."

Okay. That topic's obviously off-limits. "Why don't we take the sandwiches out to the volunteers?"

"I don't need you to come with me."

"I'll let you drive the Porsche."

"It won't go where they are. The fields are too rough."

"I'll let you drive it before I leave town. You can take a girl you like out for a spin."

He looked so torn, she almost relented. But at last he nodded. "Why do you want to go out there?"

"I want to see if Luke's okay."

"I'll take you. But you have to promise to be careful."

Roxy didn't think he meant be careful around the site of the fire. He was still worried about Luke. She reached out her hand. "I don't know if you can understand this, but I'm just as vulnerable as Luke. I really like him."

Junior searched her face. He didn't react to her statement but looked down at her sandals. "You got some sturdier shoes?" She nodded, feeling absurdly pleased by his unspoken acceptance.

He picked up the bag of sandwiches and handed it to her. "Load this into the green pickup out back. I'll get the tea."

Roxy almost floated down the hallway. It felt good to have common ground with someone who understood about Luke. And she would be seeing him very shortly.

HE LOOKED LIKE HELL, and it looked like he stood in wasteland. The fields might have been brown before but now they were blackened and lifeless. The small group of men appeared to be wilting under the weight of their protective gear and the searing temperatures.

Her clothing clung to her like she was melting. Poor Luke had sweat coming off of him in rivers, though it couldn't begin to wash the soot off his face. His smile was so white in contrast he reminded her of a jack-o'-lantern.

"Roxy, what are you doing here?" he asked. He didn't touch her but she could feel him wanting to.

She would have done the hugging despite the soot if not for the interested audience grabbing sandwiches out of the bag Junior held open. They were surrounded.

"I went to The Golden Pan. Lisa's all done in so we made the sandwiches and brought them out to you guys. You never told me you were going to fight a fire," Roxy gently scolded him.

"Lisa doesn't feel well? It's not the baby, is it?" Lisa's husband demanded hoarsely, as if he had inhaled smoke.

"Roxy," Luke said grabbing Lisa's husband by the arm, "this rash, but heroic young man is Billy, Lisa's husband."

Roxy nodded. "I met him last night."

"What's wrong with Lisa?" Billy demanded.

"She's just tired. She promised to sit down until we come back. I'm going to work another shift tonight. Junior's agreed to help me. All she'll have to do is run the register." *But I don't know how long I can stick around and do this, especially with Luke looking at me like he'd rather gobble me up than the sandwich.*

She looked down to see her sweat-streaked shirt sticking to her breasts as if she were in a wet T-shirt contest. Luke could see every scrap of lace in her bra. Billy didn't seem to notice. She crossed her arms over her chest.

"I appreciate what you're doing," Billy told her earnestly. "I know it's an imposition but Stan and Erma will be back from San Antonio soon. Then Lisa will be off until she's recovered from having the baby."

"Stan and Erma?" Roxy repeated stupidly. Luke's gaze was making it hard to think straight.

"The owners of The Golden Pan. They had to go to San Antonio because Stan has prostate cancer and he needed a treatment of some kind. Radioactive pellets, or something. The procedure is over and they're waiting for the doctors to release him."

Roxy nodded.

There was a shout from another knot of men deeper into the field and those around her hurriedly finished their tea and sandwiches. They started to file away, looking so weary Roxy's heart went out to them.

Luke put his sandwich wrapper in the trash bag hanging off of the back of Junior's pickup truck. Ignoring the few men who were finishing the tea, he reached over and held his fingers just short of her cheek. "I think you have more freckles this afternoon than you did this morning."

"I do not. I just sweated off my makeup."

"You weren't wearing makeup this morning. Just

some eyelash stuff and lipstick." He picked up his foam cup off of the back of the pickup.

"How would you know?" Roxy felt grateful she was already so hot she couldn't blush any darker. Two men avidly watched their conversation.

"I know because I stared at you all morning. I can't seem to get you out of my head."

Roxy couldn't face him in front of an audience. She lowered her head. The entire town could tell she wasn't good enough for him. Why didn't *he* get it?

After a minute he put his finger under her chin and raised it. His dark eyes gleamed. "I'll be seeing you, Miss Dallas." He saluted her with his cup of tea.

Roxy couldn't resist his baiting. "I'll be waiting, Farmer John. Take care of yourself."

"I will," he promised.

She watched him leave, wishing she felt glad he was going away—him and his absurd compliments. Junior's stare was penetrating.

"Junior, what are you looking at? We have to get back."

He took a few steps up to her. Roxy stood immobilized. What did he want? Was he going to remind her that she wasn't good enough for his hero?

"You've got it bad."

"What are you talking about?"

He reached out and touched her chin. He rubbed it firmly. Then he held his fingers before her eyes. They were covered with black soot. "It's as easy to see as this soot. You love Luke."

She didn't know what to say.

He smiled. "I guess I don't have to worry about you breaking his heart."

"Junior, you're so naive. Just because you care about someone doesn't mean you won't break their heart." *Because once Luke knows who I am he won't want me. I'll be slinking out of town with my tail between my legs. And I'm not sure I can handle it.*

She moved the tea cooler off the tailgate of the pickup, gathered up the trash bag, and then closed the tailgate. Junior watched her expectantly.

"We'd better get back," Roxy told him.

He didn't show any sign of disappointment when she didn't confide in him. He just pulled the keys out of his pocket. "Yeah, let's go home."

"This is not home." Roxy kept her expletive to herself. Teachers didn't use them if they wanted to keep their jobs. "Red Wing will never be my home. I wouldn't live in the gossip capital of the world, where young men old enough to know better spy on the sheriff just because there's nothing else to do."

He grinned unrepentantly as he started the car. They drove through dust so thick it looked like smoke until they hit the main highway again.

"You know, the town's not half bad and the sheriff's a great guy."

"The sheriff *is* a great guy."

"I mean he's a real good guy."

"You said that already."

He squirmed as if embarrassed, one hand waving

around out the open window, the other on the steering wheel. "Do you know he's got some big dogs?"

"Really?" Roxy had no intention of telling Junior that she'd been out at Luke's house this morning and met the enormous dogs.

"Yeah, they're wolfhounds. Those dogs used to belong to a man named John Lowell who killed his girlfriend, Linda, in a jealous rage."

Roxy sucked in her breath. Was this an example of what Luke meant when he'd told her about crime in a small town? "Luke knew him?"

"Luke went to school with him. They'd been casual friends. Then the man had to go to prison for the rest of his life. He pleaded with Luke to take the dogs, to give them a good home. Luke didn't hesitate. He told me that John had let his emotions get out of control but he was still a decent man. He would be paying the price for his crime for the rest of his life, but he didn't need to fret about his dogs, as well."

Roxy smoothed the hair standing up on her arms at the thought of Luke facing a man who'd killed his girlfriend. "Did Luke have to arrest that man himself? Did the man kill her in Red Wing?"

"Yes. He called Luke a few minutes after he killed her, half-crazy with grief and threatening to take his own life. Luke had to go out to his place and talk to him. He got the gun away from him and then he had to arrest him. Luke even had to tell her relatives she'd been murdered."

"I can't believe he put himself in that kind of danger." She didn't like the way she felt about Luke being in danger. She'd thought a little town like Red Wing must be pretty safe. "He told me. He said people in a small town usually hurt people they know."

Junior shrugged. "Everyone knows everyone."

"I didn't realize Luke could be in real danger."

Junior shook his head. "Didn't you just see him all rigged out in fire gear? Do you think fighting fires, answering accident calls on the highway, and responding to domestic disputes isn't dangerous?"

"No." She pulled a curl around to brush it against her cheek.

Junior caught her distress. "Hey, that's not why I told you the story."

"Then why did you tell me the story?"

"Because lots of people in town criticized him for showing John sympathy."

See, you don't want to be an outcast in this town. But something in Junior's somber retelling of the story kept her from interrupting.

"One night someone shot at the dogs and then Luke had to keep them in the house for a while. Then his house was trashed by people who didn't think he should be sympathetic toward a murderer. But he still goes to visit John. John has no family."

Roxy shifted. "I'm glad you told me. It just illustrated the huge gap between Luke and myself, which is still none of your business."

"You need to hear about Luke."

"Why? So what if Luke has a soft heart and he takes

in strays?" I am not a stray. *I'm not even good enough to qualify. At least a stray is innocent.*

"These days, there are about three guys who rotate going all the way to El Paso on visitors' day to see John."

Roxy shook her head. "Why would they do it?"

Junior tapped his finger on the steering wheel. "Because the town has a conscience. One person can set an example and people will follow."

Roxy wanted to throw up her hands in exasperation. "Why should I care about any of this?"

"I just thought you'd like to know more about Luke."

She shook her head. "I don't care. Don't tell me anything. I'm sure he's really a saint. St. Luke. Doesn't it have a nice ring? You don't have to tell me that I'm not good enough for him. I already know it."

"I didn't say you weren't good enough for him. I just don't want you to hurt him."

"Why?"

"No reason."

She flipped the curl over her shoulder. "Oh, I get it. It's okay if you pry into my personal life but I can't ask you anything."

Junior pulled his baseball cap lower on his head. "He helped me. He really helped me."

Roxy could hear the sincerity in his voice. "I'm glad. And he's lucky to have a friend like you."

"So you'll be careful? You'll stick around?"

"I can't and I won't. He knows it. I already told him

and besides, the whole town's already talking. I'm sure he's taking it into consideration."

"You didn't listen to me." He sounded exasperated.

"What? What didn't I listen to?"

"If Luke thinks you're right for him, he won't give a hoot what the town thinks. He'll just do what he needs to do."

"Like visiting the man who owned the dogs?"

"Yeah."

"And how exactly does that apply to me?"

He turned and grinned at her. "Lordy, do you sound like a teacher or what?"

She didn't have to ask him how he knew she was a teacher. Lisa no doubt told the entire town that it was on her waitressing application.

"If Luke wants you he won't let what the town thinks get in the way. The only thing stopping him will be you saying yes or no."

Roxy sucked in a breath. She'd counted on the good opinion of the town keeping Luke from making any crazy mistakes. Now she wasn't so sure. And that left only one thought on her mind.

I have to get out of here.

8

ROXY WATCHED HERSELF in the mirror as she buttoned the oversize men's shirt over her naked breasts. She felt slightly unsteady. If she hadn't already checked her sugar level she might have thought it was the diabetes. *It's not sugar; it's guilt and anticipation.* She looked deeply into her own eyes.

Am I actually bold enough to pull this off?

Maybe the question was, should she?

She couldn't tell him she was leaving tonight. He'd been fighting a fire all day. It'd be downright cruel. He probably wasn't even going to be in the mood for what she had in mind.

She turned to look at herself from the side. The shirt reached midthigh. Anyone seeing her would think she had on a bathing suit underneath the shirt. They wouldn't guess she wasn't wearing anything but her very sensitized skin.

She didn't bother with makeup. Instead she fiddled with her perfumed lotion from the drugstore.

Stop procrastinating. It was going to be a big bust if he came, read the note she'd put on the door, and then went out to the pool to discover she wasn't there. It certainly wouldn't be much of a seduction if they got their signals crossed.

And had they? She couldn't imagine she'd misunderstood. Ever since this morning he'd been bold, admitting over and over again that he wanted her. Even the message he left, telling her how late it would be before he got here, had been sweet and suggestive.

He wants me. Again. And I shouldn't need a rock to fall on my head to get it. It hasn't been that long since I've been with a man.

She gave herself one last look. The shirt was too enveloping to be sexy but the bare flesh underneath was a different story.

Having given herself the pep talk, she turned off all the lights in her room except the night-light in the bathroom, and stuck her head out the door of the motel room. The note fluttered on the orange side of the door. Nothing else moved in the moonless desert night.

In the porch lights of the motel, she counted three cars besides Luke's ancient pickup. She'd met two of the couples staying in the motel. They were well into their seventies. Not likely candidates for a swim after midnight.

If someone was already at the pool she could always pretend she'd forgotten her towel and come back to the room.

She stepped out of her door. She felt naked. It was the strangest sensation. As if she were undressed in the middle of a crowded city, not outside a little motel in the middle of nowhere. At midnight. When even the moths moved sluggishly around the porch lights, and the lizards lay languid under the cacti.

There was absolutely no one to see her.

And though she felt exposed, she also felt erotic. Like a more sophisticated version of herself. *A romantic tryst is something every woman should enjoy. I'm just behind on the romantic stuff.* Her face curved into a Mona Lisa smile. This was probably what he expected from Miss Dallas.

The cement was warm under her feet as she walked toward the pool area. She curled her toes. The air was heavy with the residue of one-hundred-twelve degree heat. Her internal temperature was rising, as well. He'd be coming soon.

She fumbled with the lock on the high privacy fence around the pool. She could see pretty well in the green light from the huge neon sign above her. The dancing cactus did interesting things to the otherwise dark landscape.

Finally she got the lock open. She opened the door and walked into the pool area, leaving the door to the privacy fence slightly ajar so he'd be able to come into the pool area. She didn't trust herself to be able to get up and let him in because her legs would surely be shaking at her audacity.

The light in the bottom of the pool made the water a lovely combination of deep green and blue. Still, it was too bright for what she had in mind. The switch was clearly marked so she walked over and switched it off.

The neon light danced on the surface of the pool. The

low hum of the pool filter seemed loud in the stillness. The height of the privacy fence and the lack of any sound or movement from outside lulled her. For this moment she existed on an island of solitude.

Her ears strained to pick up the sound of his car.

She grabbed the end of a lounge chair and then pulled it closer to the gate. She wanted him to be able to spot her, but she might need a moment to compose herself since she was hoping for the image of sophisticated city girl.

Once she was satisfied about the placement of the lounge chair she lay down. Closing her eyes, the air pressed against her, still heavy with heat. As she dozed in a soft and hazy place, memories of their dance together swirled around her.

The gate to the pool swung, the hinges making a sound that almost blended with the music in her dream. Yet she was instantly aware of her surroundings. And her nakedness. He closed the door to the privacy fence firmly enough that she heard the metal door lock engage. Did he also desire privacy?

She shivered at the thought.

"I'm glad you left a note on your door." His voice was a little deeper, huskier. A reminder that he'd had a very dangerous and difficult day. In the diffused light of the neon cactus she could see he was dressed in jeans and a T-shirt.

I should offer him sympathy and a full body massage for all of his sore muscles. If he's up for anything else I'm sure I'll discover it for myself. She smiled at the thought. Here she was thinking in sexual puns. Who would have thought she was capable of such behavior?

"What's so funny?"

"I'm just glad you came. I didn't know if you would. I thought you'd be exhausted."

"I'm exhausted, but I wanted to see you."

She gave him a slow smile. "I'm glad. I assumed that was the message you were sending me earlier. You certainly weren't shy when I brought your lunch, despite the local audience."

"I can't imagine I've given you the impression I'm shy."

She pushed a curl off her forehead. A small breeze pushed the heavy air over her body. "You blush like an altar boy. I guess I thought you might be shy."

He squatted down to the level of the lounge chair she was lying in. "I'm only tongue-tied around beautiful women."

He was looking at her so intently. Like he would rather look at her than anything else. "Then I'm glad I'm not beautiful."

"You're definitely not beautiful. In fact you look kinda like a Martian in this light."

She laughed. She couldn't help it. "You look kinda bilious yourself."

He leaned closer to her. "A man could have interesting fantasies about you in this light. He could wonder what it feels like to run his hands along your pale green skin." His smile was wide with mirth and his eyes deep with desire.

She pulled the collar of the shirt up. As if she had a prayer of resisting Luke. "A man might suffer dire consequences if he touched a woman with green skin."

He hesitated as if he were really worried. "What dire consequences?"

She stretched out her legs. The shirt rode up on her hips. "Are you brave enough to find out?"

He looked mesmerized by the tops of her thighs. "Why, what would she do to him?" His voice had thickened.

She could barely play the game for the desire scrambling her senses. Yet there was an element of truth at work. *I'm trying to warn you.*

Would he heed her warning? "Green is the color of some poisons." Roxy loosened the top button of her shirt. "Perhaps you should keep your distance."

He didn't hesitate. He ran his fingers along her leg from her knee to her thigh. Her pulse responded. Perhaps he was fearless enough.

There he hesitated. Her heart stumbled to a stop.

His eyes were on the buttons over her breasts. "I would rather die than keep my distance."

Her heart resumed, immediately going into overdrive. He reached for the top button.

She took his large hand in her own as she looked deeply into his eyes. "I wouldn't want to be the reason for your demise. At least not tonight."

With his other hand he traced the edge of the shirt where it lay on her thighs. Roxy sat rigidly, wondering if he would dare to raise the soft cotton material any higher.

"You are so incredibly desirable I don't think I could resist you even if I wanted to. Which I don't."

"Then you'll risk being tainted by my strange coloring?" She tried not to show how he was affecting her.

He ran his fingers up over the edge of the shirt and paused when he traced them to her hipbone. He'd just discovered her secret. His fingers explored from the hollow of her hip, over the very sensitive rise of her sex and then back to the other hollow. "I assure you, I'll enjoy being tainted."

She smiled. "You will enjoy it. And you won't be tainted, because you're immune. The pure of heart are always...spared." She hitched in her breath as he ran his fingers back over the hill. His exploration was making it difficult to concentrate on anything besides the urgency of her desire. He dipped into the moisture gathering beneath his fingers. "Luke." She swallowed audibly.

"I think I've discovered where you're from." He lifted the edge of the shirt from her thighs. "This terrain is definitely Venusian."

He teased the very sensitive flesh...again.

Roxy had to remind herself to keep breathing. Otherwise she was likely to turn blue from lack of oxygen. The sound of a car driving up had him pulling her shirt down over her legs. As he walked toward the gate to investigate, Roxy pulled the shirt as low as it would go.

He stood watching. Roxy followed the sound of a car

door slamming. A few minutes later the door slammed again. Luke approached her. There was the sound of a car driving off. "I guess they didn't like the price of the room," he told her.

"I suppose it was a bit pricey for illicit sex."

He came closer. He squatted right beside her. "I would have been willing to pay any price to have you."

Roxy gulped. Her feelings were so intense. She needed to lighten up for a moment. Remember this was just supposed to be a romantic liaison. Two people from different worlds, enjoying one another. "I guess you like your women...green."

He didn't reply. He didn't even smile. Instead he again reached for the buttons of the shirt over her breasts. This time she made no move to stop him. He undid the buttons with torturous patience.

Roxy wanted to scream at him to touch her.

Instead he paused.

An impossible...heart-stopping...pause.

And then he kissed her. Forever.

His hands sought her breasts until he cupped their weight in his hands. Her nipples responded. He deepened the kiss. One hand slid downward toward Venus.

Another car door slamming wrenched him away from her. He was suddenly standing and hurriedly adjusting her clothing.

"Damn," she muttered as she held the shirt together over her sensitized breasts. "Red Wing's in the middle of nowhere," she complained. "You'd think we could have a little privacy."

"I'll go see who it is." He walked the few steps toward the gate.

Roxy would have felt he was abandoning her but she knew he was only protecting her. Her flesh was thrumming with the feel of him. The taste of him. She wanted him to come back and finish his exploration.

He stood a few minutes, head cocked, obviously listening. Car doors closed again, an engine started and Luke came back toward her. But he stopped short, leaning against the fence. "They took the room but they're seniors and I doubt they'll be using the pool tonight. It's after midnight."

"Seems like a lot of traffic," Roxy complained. She stretched her arm so the shirt bared most of one breast. She no longer felt shy, just hungry for him.

"This place does have a certain atmosphere." His voice was nonchalant, but his eyes caressed her chest. His smile was wide and...green.

She laughed. "Go ahead and grin. But I must say you look pretty strange. I think this must be some kind of alien planet." She unbuttoned the shirt all the way down baring all of her sensitized flesh. Her nipples stood at attention. "Why don't you come and explore the uncharted hills and valleys?"

The door to a motel room slammed in the distance. "I think they're on their way to bed," he observed helpfully without any indication he'd noticed that she'd bared herself to him.

"You're killing me, Farmer John," she groaned.

"I hope so."

"Why?"

"Because, you're killing me, too."

"So, what do you think they're doing?" She slid her hand south to stroke the red curls she ached for him to touch.

"I think he's taking off his shirt," he said as he pulled his T-shirt out of the waistband of his jeans. He took a few steps toward her, dropping the shirt carelessly on the cement.

Roxy watched avidly. She reached up to touch her aching nipples. The muscles in his shoulders made him look a hundred feet across. Such male beauty literally stole her breath away. "Then what?" she asked.

He paused to unsnap his jeans. "He'll be pulling off his pants." He pulled down the jeans.

"You aren't wearing anything under your jeans," she pointed out. Almost blushing at his blatant desire to have her. She wanted him, too. Intensely. She rubbed her legs together.

"The same reason you aren't wearing anything under your shirt. I guess we both knew what we wanted." His husky voice went through her.

She held her hands out to him. "Come here. Please." How could he just stand there, sexy and naked?

He certainly wanted her. The evidence was quite prominent. She patted the lounge chair. "Come and tell me the intimate details of your desire." In another place it might have been corny but here, tonight, she meant every word of it. "Please touch me," she begged.

"Not here." He came closer.

"Not here," she echoed, stupidly.

"In the water. I'm parched." He squatted beside her.

She licked her lips. She, too, was dying of thirst. If only he would kiss her.

"I've been fighting a fire."

"Yes," she breathed. In the act of drawing the edges of her shirt together he brushed her nipples.

"I want to plunge in."

"Oh, yes." She kissed his neck as he lifted her to her feet.

"Deeply." He guided her to the pool's edge. "And I'm going to take you with me," he growled as he swept her up and carried her into the water.

There was no shock descending into the water—it was the same temperature as the air. The shirt immediately took on weight—weight that hung on already sensitized parts of her body. He took her deeper. She shivered. The water lifted the shirt, rubbing the heavy cotton against her nipples. Small waves lapped against her in a seductive rhythm.

Then he stopped. He pushed her up against the side of the pool where she could barely stand. Whether it was the depth or the lack of strength in her legs, she didn't care. He held her effortlessly, kissing her.

She kissed him back. Her legs dangled uselessly. Every part of her was weightless. She clung to the wall of his chest. The water enveloped her, stimulating her most intimate desires. She drank it in, a passive, willing recipient.

He wasn't passive. He touched her, tantalized her,

running his roughened fingers over her nipples, gripping her bottom, kneading until she keened. "Luke, please. Luke," she cried.

He pushed her into the wall of the pool, the points of her shoulders scraping the side through the shirt. He pinned her with his strength, burying his fingers deeply into her slick body until she arched against him. He took her scream into his own mouth.

Then he thrust inside her with raw force and heat. Small waves took up their rhythm. The endless slick friction between them propelled her higher. She writhed against him, riding the crest into the heart of the wave, and then she floated away.

As he held her securely in the shelter of his arms, she laid her head against his shoulder in surrender.

"Oh, Luke," she sighed.

ROXY WOBBLED THROUGH the gate and onto the sidewalk partially supported by Luke's strong arm.

She felt so relaxed. She probably had a big dopey smile on her face. If any of these senior citizens happened to be wandering around in the middle of the night they wouldn't have much trouble guessing what they'd been doing.

But they couldn't know how wonderful he'd made her feel. Only the warm support of his arm around her shoulder kept her tethered to the sidewalk. *If he wasn't holding me I would just drift away.*

Yet her eyelids drooped. She wanted to resist. Stay awake and memorize this feeling to take away for all the lonely tomorrows. She blinked rapidly to keep her eyes clear.

"Are you tired?" he asked solicitously.

"I think I could lie down on the cement and sleep like a stone."

"I'm feeling relaxed myself," he commented mildly.

Her head was almost too heavy to lift so she watched the pattern of water drops she was leaving on the cement below her slow-moving feet. The wet shirt stuck coolly against her oversensitized skin, warmed only where he was touching her. The edge of the material flapped against her thighs. She stopped to feel the droplets run down her legs, over her feet and onto the warm cement. She curled her toes.

"Hey, girl, don't stop. We'll both end up camped out on this walkway. I don't think Lloyd would appreciate it. He's likely to charge us."

"Okay," she sighed. "I'm walking." She straightened up, looking fondly into his handsome face. Of course it was bile green. "You know, I'm becoming fond of this color. I'll have to get some of those colored lightbulbs when I get home. They'll remind me of our time together."

Luke felt like he was walking along a sidewalk full of land mines. "Are you planning on going home soon? School doesn't start for another month." He hoped he sounded casual enough. She acted as skittish as a wild horse when they talked about her life and he didn't want to spook her. She would run for the hills if she understood how he felt about her. And he had every intention of roping her in.

"Teachers have to be at school about two weeks early and I have some other things I've got to do."

She pushed away from him. He expected it. She was certainly independent. That and everything else about her intrigued the hell out of him. He wanted to handcuff her to his side so she would never get away. "Dallas isn't so far away. I think I can arrange to visit from time to time."

"You'd come and see me?" She sounded half-strangled. She began to walk faster, though they were moving at a snail's pace.

He almost laughed at her panic. He wondered what she was hiding. When they were making love it was the only time he felt she was being totally honest with him. She gave everything of herself in a fashion that left him breathless. And susceptible. He had to find out what she was hiding.

Had she come out of an abusive situation? She didn't seem the type. But there was a depth to her that suggested she'd done her share of hard times. More than her fair share. It really bothered him to think someone had hurt her.

"Do you have someone special waiting for you at home?" He knew he sounded as helpless as buzzard's prey. There had been no hard promises between them. He had a feeling any promises he might make would only cause her to run faster. Not to mention that he'd claimed to have been engaged just days before. She wouldn't believe him even if he tried to make a commitment. And, really, could he honestly be sure of what he felt?

"My father. I have to get home to my father. He'll be worried."

"No, that's not what I meant." No woman who looked as good as she did could be single. She had to have a significant other.

"I have lots of friends depending on me but I don't have anyone...special. No romantic entanglements."

Is that what he was? An entanglement? It might be hard for her to see herself settling for a man from such a small town. He didn't intend to give her a choice. "I'm glad. I enjoy being your...entanglement."

She stopped. She leaned closer to him. "I enjoyed it, too. As a matter of fact I can't think of anything I'd rather do than tangle with you. Are you planning on staying with me tonight? I don't want you to drive home if you're tired. And Millie's already gossiping about us so a bit more can't hurt anything."

It was a nice thought, but he was all done in. He gently pushed her along to her room. "I have to go home and rest up. I wanted to take you for a horseback ride tomorrow. We'll head for the salt pond after we get hot."

"Shall I pack a swimsuit?"

"I'm kinda partial to the one you've got on under that shirt, and we'll have all the privacy we could want."

She drifted close enough to grab on to his upper arm. "Sounds great. But I'll need a rubdown after all that riding."

"I think I can manage it." Her scent drifted up to him. Suddenly he was wondering if he were really all done in.

She tripped on a seam in the sidewalk. He steadied her. "You seem just a little tipsy."

She pulled away abruptly. "I'm not drunk!"

He grabbed her arm firmly and pulled her to his chest. "Shh." He stroked her hair and whispered in her ear. "I'm enjoying the idea of you being drunk on our lovemaking. A man's ego needs to be stroked on a fairly regular basis."

She was smiling again, her teeth green in her face. Unexpectedly she reached between them to touch him through his jeans. "I guess that's not all that needs a good stroking."

"Now, who has the bawdy sense of humor? Aren't you the lady who was outraged by the insinuation she might be tipsy on lovemaking? Have you no shame?"

"The only real shame is how exhausted you must be from fighting fires all day. I guess you should go home and rest." She pulled away from him.

He nodded, trying to convince himself. He couldn't stay the night. It was just too blatant. His relationship shouldn't be the town's business. He served these people. He didn't have to be served up by them, as well.

When they reached her room he took the keys from her and then opened the door. There was just enough light shining from the bathroom night-light for him to see that the room was tidy.

"Is there anything I can get for you? Have you eaten recently?" he asked her. "Do you need some juice?"

"I'm fine," she said absently as she made her way to the large bed. She took off the clinging shirt and hung it on the back of a chair next to the bed. Then she scrambled under the covers.

He looked away from the bed. He rubbed his hands together so he wouldn't be tempted to put them anywhere he shouldn't.

"Why don't you pull down this bedspread? I'm burning up," Roxy requested as she stretched under the covers.

He moved toward the bed as if it held a rattlesnake. He pulled the heavy bedspread down. Then he snatched his hands back and took several steps toward the relative safety of the door.

"I think this is where we started this morning." She poked one of those long legs out from under the sheet.

He shook his head. "No way. No way am I going to play this game. I've got to go home."

"All I ask is that you give me a good-night kiss." She pursed her lips like a little girl.

"No, Roxy. I'll come and get you tomorrow. I'll be by around ten. Get some sleep."

"You kissed me last night." She pouted.

"You grow more dangerous every day." He turned around and then he let himself out of the room, locking the door with a firm click.

9

SEVERAL HOURS LATER she woke with tears streaming down her face. She didn't have to strain to remember the details of the nightmare. She'd been chasing Mick and she couldn't find him. She'd wanted him. More than a drink, more than her life. But when she'd found him he became Luke. Luke rejected her because of her past. The townspeople laughed at her everywhere she went, pointing as if they were all in a bad movie.

"It was just a dream, nothing but a stupid dream." The sound of her voice should have been soothing, yet it barely permeated her grief. Though absurd, the dream had felt so real. Whom did she want more than a drink?

Luke?

When had he become an addiction?

She picked up the phone, concentrating on Mick. Once she knew he was fine she could shrug off the dream and all it implied. She dialed the direct line to the guest suite.

Mick picked up. "Hello?"

"What the heck are you doing up?"

"You sound like a damn schoolteacher. You don't even swear anymore."

"I *am* a damn schoolteacher."

"I'm sitting by your pool." She could hear the smile in his voice.

"With the phone in hand? It's three o'clock in the morning." She didn't want to ask him if he were sober. She didn't want to assume the worst. He sounded okay.

"I don't want to miss any calls from Joey. He's always been a night owl. What are *you* doing up at three o'clock in the morning?"

"I had a nightmare. I couldn't find you. It scared me." *And I wasn't good enough for Luke. Why does it terrify me when I've known it all along?*

"Roxy, I'm fine," he said patiently.

"I thought you'd be asleep and I'd leave a message for you to call me."

"I'm okay. How's the digs in Red Dog?"

"Red Wing."

"Okay. Red Wing."

"The motel is decorated in orange and brown. Luke says the guy who owns it is color blind. The maid here is the gossip queen of the universe and there's a green neon sign out front that gives the landscape a distinctly Martian aura after dark."

"Sounds like a McMurtry novel. Who's Luke?"

"The sheriff."

His voice turned serious. "You've been in trouble and you didn't tell anyone?"

"I have *not* been in trouble. He's just protective of his town. I met him in the local diner where I'm waitressing." She pulled a piece of hair over her shoulder to rub it against her cheek.

"Waitressing? Again? I thought you'd sworn off that job when you quit working for us. Remember how it used to drive me crazy when the guys came on to you?"

"I couldn't stand when you guys hovered over me—even thought it was sweet. Besides, the hardest thing they sell in this restaurant is Dr. Pepper. How's Joey?"

"Joey seems embarrassed, ashamed and even a little grateful."

"Good. When does he get out of the hospital?"

"Tomorrow. That's why I'm sitting here, still sober. I plan to take care of him."

"You need to go to AA. They can help you stay sober."

"One brother in AA at a time is good enough. Anyway I've cut back to beer. It takes a long time to get drunk on beer. Have you been thinking about David?"

"I have." There was a catch in her voice.

"You don't have to talk about him."

She sighed. "You know, it's funny. I've talked about David with my shrink for years. I thought I'd talked through it, but apparently I hadn't because his death was the first thing I thought of when I heard about Joey."

"That's what you said. It seems pretty normal to me."

"I told a story about him today. It was a funny thing he used to do when we were kids. He used to dance around trying to flatten my soufflé."

"Your what?"

"You know the puffy dessert. He used to try to make it go flat because I didn't want to share," she sniffed.

"Are you crying?"

He sounded nervous. Mick always lost his cool when a woman started to cry. "I'm not crying."

"You know, only rich kids know how to make soufflé. The rest of us can't even spell it."

She laughed.

"That's better. No crying allowed. You wouldn't want to make an old man like me break down, would you?"

"Don't worry, they're good tears. I don't mind remembering and crying about the good things. In fact, I'm going to make a habit of it."

"It sounds okay," he told her cautiously, "except for the waterworks. When are you coming home?"

"Soon. I'll be home soon."

"That's good. I thought I might have to come and get you."

"Tell my dad I said hello."

"Okay."

"Mick? Get some sleep. Promise me you'll go to bed now?"

"It's hard to sleep. It's easier when you're loaded. The nights are longer without the booze."

"I remember when I had the same problem. Get into the hot tub."

"Are you kidding? It's still eighty-some degrees here."

"I know. The heat will zap you. You'll fall into your

cool sheets with great relief. Try it, kid. What've you got to lose?"

"Okay, but I still think you're crazy."

"Then nothin's changed. See you soon."

SHE PUT THE RECEIVER gently on the cradle.

I am crazy. Crazy for staying in Red Wing where I don't belong.

The dream had been so real.

She wasn't the one who grew more dangerous every day they were together. Luke was the one. He was every bit as addictive as alcohol and that scared her to death. *I can't allow myself to become obsessed again when I can't handle the obsession I'm already fighting.*

Tears ran down her cheeks. Tomorrow she would pick up her car. She had to go home before she got in deeper. She couldn't ride off into the sunset with Farmer John; it wouldn't be fair to him. He didn't know what he would be getting and she wasn't strong enough to admit how terribly low she'd once sunk. He'd turn away from her if he knew. It would destroy everything she'd fought for these past years.

What if she were to tell him about her past, give him a chance?

But he was his job. An elected official. What would the town of Red Wing say about their beloved sheriff being with someone like her?

She had to leave this town tomorrow. It was for the best. If he had to choose between her and his job, she was certainly no bargain. She laid her head down on her pillow and spent the rest of the night flaying herself with torturous visions of past crimes, the tears flowing freely onto her pillow.

FOR BREAKFAST she'd ordered coffee she couldn't swallow and a meal she hadn't touched. "I want you to take me to pick up my car," she told him. The words tasted all wrong, which was ironic, since she loved her Porsche. "I've got to go home," she insisted more to herself than to him.

He raised the fork to his mouth as if she'd just commented on the weather. She'd picked the diner as the ideal place to tell him she wasn't going horseback riding with him. It seemed best to tell him in a public place where he wouldn't try to convince her to stay. She was afraid he might touch her.

"Why do you have a hankering to go home all of a sudden?" he inquired casually. "Can't you stay the rest of the weekend?"

Was it Sunday? He had her all mixed up, as if she were drinking again. She opened her mouth to give him an excuse and then shut it. She didn't want to lie to him.

"You do have a reason, don't you?" he asked. "Because it seems to me things are going pretty well between us."

She blushed. Pretty well? Is that what he called how things were going? Blazing out of control was more like it. And she'd only known him three days. She needed to fight this fire or get burned, badly.

"It's for the best." She picked up a biscuit so she had

something to do with her hands. "This thing between us is more than I bargained for. I have to go home and get my head on straight before we make a costly mistake."

He ate his bacon in small economical bites. She tried not to watch him. Then he took a sip of his coffee. He looked at her, studying her intently.

She buried her nose in her cup of coffee. She thought she knew what he was seeing. Her eyelids were puffy from crying. Her nose was red and the circles under her eyes looked like swipes of misplaced mascara. She'd been such a mess she hadn't even attempted to cover the ravages of a night spent arguing with herself. It would have been futile.

"Okay."

Her hand jerked hard enough to spill the coffee. "Ow! Darn!" She swiped at the dribble of hot liquid that had landed on her thigh.

"Are you all right?" He shoved his napkin at her.

"Yes," she said mopping the coffee off the outside of the mug and her thigh. "I'm just a klutz."

"You're not a klutz," he said mildly. "You're one of the most graceful women I've ever seen. I love to watch you gesture with your hands, or walk on those endless legs."

She just kept from slamming the coffee cup down on the table. "Why are you doing this to me?"

"Doing what?"

"How can you sit there so calmly and compliment

me, when I just told you I have to go home? And you said okay, like I asked you to pass me the sugar."

"Don't think that your going home is going to end this," he told her mildly.

She shook her head in disbelief. "Think again, Farmer John. This is never going to work."

"You go home if you have to. The doc told me about your kind of diabetes. It gets worse when you're under strain. Go home and take care of yourself. When you've thought about what you want, call me. I'll come and visit."

"This is not about the diabetes. I'm not sick. I'm being logical. I can't stay here, and you'd hate Dallas." It was the least of her concerns, but any excuse would do.

"I want to spend time with you. I think what we feel for one another deserves a try."

She sniffed, "You don't fight fair."

He smiled. "I only fight fair when I'm on the job."

She tried to keep the tears from falling in earnest. "Can we get out of here before I make a spectacle of myself?"

He rose to his feet, threw some bills on the table. They walked to the door and then went outside. The heat hit her like a wall.

"I don't want you to worry about Lisa. I'll find someone to waitress for her."

"I guess you're not up on the latest gossip. The people who own the diner are back in town."

He gave her one of his intense looks. "I've been preoccupied lately. Is Stan feeling better?"

"From what I understood he's doing pretty well."

"Medical science is amazing. Just a few days ago he was radioactive."

For some reason the thought of being radioactive reminded her of the green light at the pool. Would she ever forget the way Luke touched her? Suddenly she felt heat on the inside as well as the outside.

"What are you thinking?"

"Nothin'." *He couldn't tell she was thinking about making love just by looking at her. He couldn't.*

He escorted her to his truck. "It's those kinds of thoughts I'm counting on. I think you'll break down and call despite all our differences. We have something between us. Something strong."

"I don't know what you're talking about." She opened the door and gingerly climbed in the pickup. All the metal surfaces were burning. He stood there watching her. Smirking.

"I think you'll go home and when the lights are low you'll remember the way it feels when I come deep inside of you and you fall apart in my arms."

The windows were open to the dusty wind. But it didn't do a thing to cool the hot desire rolling through her. *Down, girl. You made a decision last night and it was the right decision.*

Fortunately he left her window and went around to climb inside of the pickup.

He was right. She would miss him. And not just when the lights were low. She would miss the deep rasping of his voice when he gave her those incredible matter-of-fact compliments that spoke directly to her soul.

He started the pickup and then drove out of the driveway toward Larry's gas station.

She realized he had indeed become an obsession. She had to escape. "I have a life. If I call to find out how you're doing it will just be a courtesy on my part." *I won't tell you I'm dying for the sound of your voice to wash over me. I won't tell you I'm lying awake.*

"I'd appreciate your courtesy. You'll let me know if there's anything I can do for you?" His voice was matter-of-fact. She wanted to strangle him.

They pulled up to the gas station. Her Porsche sat alone in the back, its deep yellow paint job reflecting the harsh sunlight.

"It's a cute little car. Kinda feisty. Reminds me of you."

"My father said something similar when he gave it to me as a gift for a special occasion." *Three-hundred-sixty-five days sober. It was a bigger celebration for us than any holiday.*

"How do you fit those legs inside such a little car?"

She tried not to blush. "The seat goes really far back. *You'd* fit if you want to drive it a ways."

He looked at her. "You wouldn't mind? You seem to be in quite a hurry."

She knew she was stalling, and she was going to pay for every minute they spent together. Still, she wanted a few more minutes. "I just need to get a bottle of water from inside." She dug around in the backpack she'd bought at the market, until she came up with her keys. Avoiding the warmth of his callused skin, she gingerly placed them in his outstretched hand.

She climbed out of his pickup as fast as she could with her dignity intact. She hurried into the gas station, which wasn't air-conditioned, yet she loitered, trying to make it look like she was trying to make a selection from the limited variety of snacks.

Through the window she watched Luke lower himself into her car. He didn't look out of place. It was strange how right he looked in her world. Eventually the curious gaze of Larry, the gas station guy, sent her reluctantly to the register.

"I guess you and the sheriff came for your car," Larry commented as he rang up the gas for her car, the water, and then counted out her change one coin at a time. Roxy didn't care if it took all day.

"Yeah, thanks for keeping it safe for me."

Larry took off his cap and wiped the sweat beading his pink brow above his farmer's tan. "I didn't mind. In just a few days, I got more business in sodas and snacks than I usually have in a month. Those kids love your little car."

"All kids love sports cars."

The sound of the Porsche's engine revving interrupted them. Roxy looked around. *Who does Luke think he is, revving my car like he's in the Indy 500?*

"Guess the sheriff likes it, too." Larry picked up an old can from the counter and spat into it.

She pretended she didn't notice the bits of tobacco

mixed in with his white beard stubble. He looked like he'd trimmed it with a kitchen knife. She smiled a big phony smile. "I think your sheriff is as bad as the kids."

"I guess the sheriff's a bit like a kid." Larry gestured with the can. "But he's a decent man. The town wouldn't be the same without him looking after things.

"Take him a Dr. Pepper." Roxy tried not to cringe when she saw Larry sling his spit can in her direction, obviously pointing just behind her at the refrigerator holding rows of soft drinks. "He drinks the stuff like it's water."

Luke revved the Porsche again. Roxy thought she might strangle him. "He can buy his own Dr. Pepper," she told Larry. "Thanks again for your help."

"No problem. You come back now." Larry turned away. Roxy stood, hesitating. Larry was much safer than Luke. However, it seemed Larry was finished talking. He'd put down his can and picked up a grease-stained copy of *Harry Potter and the Order of the Phoenix*, effectively dismissing her. Roxy sighed and walked out of the station.

Luke had pulled up the Porsche next to his pickup. It was idling and he was fishing for something in the bed of the truck. Roxy went around to the passenger side door, already regretting she'd told Luke he could drive the Porsche.

"Why don't I wait here?" She directed her voice toward the pickup but he'd already moved to the back of the Porsche where he was putting something in the trunk.

It was probably her bag. He was ever the gentleman. Even if it meant she was leaving him.

She looked longingly toward Larry's.

"You want to wait with Larry? It's hot as Hades in there. He doesn't like to spend the money on air-conditioning. Says he sells more cold drinks that way." Luke patiently waited beside her car.

She stood, indecisive. *I've got to be stronger than this.* "Okay. I'm coming." She walked toward her car. *I can let him go. I've only known him for three days.*

And it was killing her. *I want to know he's suffering,* said the voice of the illogically feminine Roxy. It was no wonder men didn't think women made any sense.

Luke grinned at her as she approached. He looked just like a teenager. "Ready to go?" he asked.

Roxy nodded. She walked to the passenger side door and hesitated only a moment before opening it. What was she doing? She should insist he get out, and then take this car and point it east. Only he looked up at her with a grin so wide he was endearing, like a little boy.

Her answering grin was weak as she settled in on her side of the car. The intimacy of the confining space enveloped her. His elbow could brush the side of her breast if he just reached out to adjust the dial on the radio. She didn't know if she wanted him to adjust the radio or not. Every time he touched her it became easy. There were no doubts. She wanted that, *and* she wanted to get the hell out of Red Wing. "Where are we going?"

"Remember that lonely stretch of road?"

I will never forget it. "Yeah, I remember."

He left Red Wing with a couple of smooth turns and then they were driving along the highway.

"I like this car. She handles beautifully." He didn't seem to notice the tight confines. Instead he pressed on the accelerator, fiddled with the gearshift and soon had the powerful engine humming. The car accelerated smoothly.

He has that effect on me, too. Needing to concentrate on something besides how close they were, Roxy complained. "How fast are you going? I hope you get a ticket."

He turned just enough to show her the huge grin on his face. "I don't think so. I have my badge with me."

"Isn't that a bit hypocritical?" So he wasn't as straight as he appeared. Instead of making him less attractive it made him more attractive. Her mind conjured up all kinds of ways they could be naughty together.

"And your point is..." he said, interrupting her fantasies.

"Is this what you do in your squad car when you get out here on these wide-open roads? Or is it only when you're with me? I'd hate to think I'm corrupting the law in Red Wing, especially since I've already put your job in jeopardy."

"You haven't put my job in jeopardy."

She lay back in her seat concentrating on the empty road flying by them in a blur. Her stomach turned with all kinds of conflicting emotions. How could she leave him? How could she stay?

Because this exhilarating speed represented their relation-

ship. Like they were going along at over a hundred miles an hour. Every time they made love it was instant internal combustion. Yet they didn't really know each other. Not what was actually under the hood. She might drive a Porsche but she wasn't like the Porsche, all polished and wonderful. She was like his old pickup.

How could he be so confident? What would he think if she told him everything? *Our relationship would turn into a flaming wreck.*

Open your mouth and say something pointless and inane before you tell him something you'll both regret, and ruin these last moments with him. "I love this car…it's become a symbol of all the things I've accomplished in the last two years."

He slowed the car. "Your dad must be pretty proud of you."

"He is."

"What was the occasion? Did you graduate from college or what?"

Her hands went cold. She rubbed them back and forth on the denim material of her shorts. She couldn't tell him. She didn't have the guts for it. "I finished a few things. I graduated. I got a job. Things finally came together for me." *And I sweated each and every day thinking I might stumble and lose it all.*

"I think it's wonderful. Did he wrap up the keys or put a huge ribbon on the car?"

"He wrapped the keys in a box from a jeweler I love. It fooled me until I opened it to find the key ring with the Porsche symbol on it. The car was parked right outside the window of the restaurant where we were sitting. I'd already admired it twice during dinner."

"You must have felt like a kid getting a puppy for Christmas."

Better. The car was a symbol of earning her father's respect. Nothing could compare. Nothing but deserving Luke.

"Well, what did it feel like?" he prodded gently.

"It was thrilling because he recognized how hard I'd worked and respected me for it. I cried so hard he had to drive it. He even had it custom painted in my favorite color."

"I can't say I'd go for this color. But it's sassy, so it suits you." He slowed the car a bit more.

She wondered where they were going. There was nothing on the horizon except a bedraggled tree a few miles ahead.

"Are all your daddy's gifts so lavish? Do you have a ten-car garage at home?"

"What are you trying to ask me, Farmer John?"

"Are you rich, lady?" he teased, yet a serious note sounded loud and clear.

"Yep, trust fund and all. Does it bother you?" She sounded casual. She wished it didn't matter. It was just another disparity between them.

"Sure, but it won't stop me from coming to Dallas after you."

Her heart leaped. "Are you sure?"

"Will I have to scale high walls, beat off attack dogs,

vault alarm systems and challenge uptight boyfriends with memberships at the local country clubs?"

She could picture him coming to Dallas. It was a nice thought. Her apartment would surprise him with its simplicity. Her dad's house, on the other hand, was pretty much as he'd described it. "You'll have to fight them off in that order. Especially the attack dogs. My father's also pretty formidable. He'll ask for your stock portfolio."

He slowed the car even further. He was smiling again. "It won't take him long to go over the portfolio but I think I'm up to the other challenges."

He pulled off of the road onto the paved shoulder. He coasted along until they reached the scrubby little tree. "Ah, shade. This mesquite tree is the only real tree for miles in either direction." Nudging right up under the tree he shifted the car into Park.

"You're not going to stop the engine and turn off the air-conditioning are you?" Roxy knew she sounded panicked. He was downright crazy. Just three days ago hadn't he reprimanded her for sitting in a car in the middle of the hottest summer on record? And the midmorning heat was already fading the sky and knocking on the windows. "I don't think this qualifies as shade in the real world."

"Out here you have to take what you can get." He engaged the parking brake.

"It's over a hundred degrees out there, Luke. I can afford the gas. Just leave the engine on, please? You wouldn't want me to get overheated and dehydrated. I might end up in the clinic again."

"Don't tempt me. You'd be surprised what I'd do to keep you around." He left the car running. "I'm only sparing you because you hate needles." He opened his door and slung one long leg out of the low car.

"Where are you going?" Roxy could just imagine him settling down on the side of the road underneath the pitiful excuse for a tree. He'd probably brought his own blanket. What had he put in her trunk? He couldn't mean to seduce her out in the middle of the desert?

He turned back to her, moving as if he had all the time in the world. "I could use a drink, do you want one?"

I want a drink every day, that's why I'm trying so hard to tell you goodbye. "I don't want anything."

He just sat there with the door open. He was watching her intently and she was infinitely tired of that look, which told her he was trying to read between the lines.

You can look all you want, but I'm not giving up any incriminating evidence, Sheriff. "Well, what are you waiting for? Shut the door before all of the cool air escapes into the desert."

"This isn't a desert. You go a few hundred miles farther west and you'll see desert. This place is downright green in comparison."

"You have your definition of green and I have mine."

He bent down and examined the dashboard on his side. "Where's your trunk release?"

"It's over there." She gestured at the little lever. "It has a picture."

"Come closer and show me."

"I can't get much closer. This is a very small car if you hadn't noticed." The close confines had been driving her crazy for the last half hour and he'd been completely unaware. She should be insulted. He'd been mesmerized by the Porsche.

"I noticed. That's why I need a Dr. Pepper. If I don't do something with my hands, I'm going to put them all over you. And you don't seem to want that right now."

Roxy shivered. He was right and yet the possibilities were downright intriguing. She'd never made love in the Porsche.

Focus, girl. You need to get away from here. Remember? You're planning to run away.

He looked at her intently. "Am I mistaken about your intentions? You still plan to go home today?"

Her neck felt stiff, but she managed a nod. She had to go home. She owed it to him not to screw up his life and his chances for reelection.

He stood up. Then he gently shut the car door.

I have to figure out how to tell him goodbye. I have to go home before we both end up getting hurt. I have to do the right thing. This time I can't fail.

Luke opened the door and then reached across to hand her a glass bottle. Then he climbed into the car and shut the door. Roxy looked down at the orange juice. She bit her lip to keep from crying. He was always taking care of her. His innate kindness made her heart ache. "I don't need orange juice. I'm not sick." It came out harsh.

"I also have bottled water and Dr. Pepper." He popped the tab on his can, unconcerned about her sudden temper.

"I told you I don't want anything." *I don't want to hurt you. Take away your life. Can't you understand?*

"I guess this is goodbye. For a bit." He reached out as if he might touch her and she jerked out of his way. Then he put his hands up as if in surrender.

"Yes." She turned away and then rested her face against the window, as far away from him as the limited space would allow her to get. *It's goodbye forever.*

He put both hands around the can. "I want your address and phone number. I've got a few days of vacation coming, but I'll have to put stuff in order before I come."

"I don't think this is a good idea."

"What?"

"You coming to see me." Roxy refused to look at him. "We are from two different worlds."

"I won't allow you to walk out of my life. I don't want to use my job as an excuse to access information you should give me yourself, but I don't see any other option. I feel too strongly about you just to let go."

Roxy closed her eyes. A background check. He was going to do a background check on her. Let him. It'd be easier than trying to tell him herself. "You're not being fair," she heard herself say.

"In our situation I can't play fair. I want you. I'm going to fight for you."

"What, is this the dark ages? You're not some knight trying to win my heart. I know what I need, and you can't be a part of my life after today."

Don't say anything, Luke cautioned himself. *Be patient.* He'd just let her run until she tired herself and then he'd rope the filly in a bit. Eventually, maybe, she'd get used to him.

"Luke, I never made you any promises."

Don't ruin it by shifting into emotional high gear. He knew all he had to do was touch her and she'd fold. Right now she exuded so much painful tension he could barely take it.

"Just take us back to Red Wing. Please. I want to go home." Her voice was thick with tears.

"I want to sit a moment." His hands shook with the frustration of wanting to hold her, comfort her.

"Why?" she cried out. "There's nothing more to say!"

"I've got things I want to say."

"No, don't try to convince me. It's better this way. Quicker. You have your career to think about."

He didn't look at her. He wondered if there were tears welling up in those crystal-blue eyes. "What does my career have to do with anything?" he asked carefully.

"The whole town must think poorly of you when you've dumped your long-term girlfriend to have a meaningless affair with a woman who just blew into town for a few days. It can't help your reelection chances," she sniffed.

"You've stated the situation as badly as you possibly could, making my actions sound utterly irresponsible, but I think my job's pretty secure."

"If you go back to Carla, they'll forgive you," she sniffed louder.

He finally looked at her. Her nose was red. Her eyes were wide. She fiddled with that glorious hair. He wanted nothing more than to kiss her senseless. She said the most irritating shit. "I'm not going back to Carla. And I won't put our time together in the worst light. You may have blown into town for a short time but despite having no ties to our town, you helped Lisa out at The Golden Pan. You brought sandwiches out to the men at the fire. You didn't just lounge around the pool at the Cozy Daze thumbing your nose at the local scenery. You got to know folks. I think you'd be surprised at what people think of you."

"I want to go back to Red Wing. I have to start for home."

He shrugged. "Okay. You win. I'm going to take you back. Along the way, I want you to think about what I said. I want you to consider telling me whatever it is that's hurting you. The only stumbling blocks to you and me having a relationship are that you're married or a bank robber." He smiled at her. "And I might even look past the bank robber part."

He turned on the ignition. The car purred to life. *Too bad women aren't as easy to handle as machinery.*

"If I think about what you said, will you promise not to run a background check on me? I'd feel violated. And I don't want you to come to Dallas until I'm ready to see you."

"You have to promise to call me in two weeks, even if you only want to say goodbye. And you have to speak to *me.* You could also call me when you get safely into Dallas. I don't want to have to put out an APB."

"I'm a big girl. I can get home by myself."

"It's the big girls who get into the most trouble."

"Okay, I promise."

"Fine." He concentrated on the road. He had to be satisfied with the promise of a phone call.

If she didn't call, well, he had her tag numbers memorized. He didn't always fight fair. Not when it was something he wanted as badly as he wanted Roxanne Adams.

10

ONCE IN HER CAR and pointed east, Roxy congratulated herself on having the resolve to drive away, at the same time wondering how it could be so hard to leave him behind.

Each mile lasted forever. About forty miles from Red Wing, she got off the highway at the first little mom-and-pop store she saw. She got a drink and then visited the rest room. Out in the parking lot she paced, under the pretext of stretching her legs, until her hair stuck to the side of her neck and she thought she'd wilt in the heat.

She repeated her pit stop routine about every forty minutes to an hour as she came to the small sad towns with boarded-up buildings and empty homes. She was just contributing to the local economies, she told herself.

Back in the car, Roxy looked at her sunburned nose in the rearview mirror and told herself she *should* buy sunscreen at the next stop.

Yeah, it will give you another excuse.

Roxy looked at the ragamuffin in the mirror. *I can stop if I want to.*

The next town showed signs of prosperity. She stopped anyway. *I just need some sunscreen and a baseball cap.* She'd just gotten out of her car when a rancher got out of an old pickup just as dilapidated as Luke's. Roxy jumped back into her car and drove away. She fiddled with the radio and cried along with the country and western songs.

Gradually the scenery changed. Trees dotted the landscape of rolling hills and tall green grass. Somehow the sky seemed diminished by all of the greenery she'd once loved. It just didn't look right anymore. Her heart burned and so did her stomach. *It's all those sugary things you had to drink.* She turned into a gas station to get some antacids. They didn't help.

About an hour from home she turned in at another rest stop. This time she sat for about an hour with the car running and her heart and soul at war with one another. She turned off the highway but only ended up making a circle. With the Porsche pointed west, the miles seemed to fly.

This was the worst idea in the world. *I can't believe you're going back,* she told herself, taking a hand off of the wheel to bite her nails and worry her cuticles.

But he had something she needed. It would pass. What was another couple of days until she discovered he had some really annoying habits and then she'd happily head for home.

You can't afford another addiction, her conscience told her. *And you can't afford to hurt anyone, especially a good man like Luke.*

She rubbed her stomach. She just wanted a few more

days. Then she'd go back to Dallas, go to school, and forget she ever heard of a place called Red Wing.

She was sure the good people of Red Wing would pretend nothing had ever happened. Carla would make sure of it. Luke would be safe. He'd kept telling her the town would forgive and forget. Besides, they'd never find out anything about her past. She was just a mysterious woman who passed through town once upon a time in July.

The little car raced toward the setting sun.

This is a terrible idea, she thought.

IT WAS STILL HOT, despite the fact that the sun had been down for an hour, when she found herself standing on his porch. At least the dogs didn't appear to be loose. *What am I doing back here?* She'd wasted an entire day.

She knocked hesitantly on the door to his house.

The dogs barked from somewhere in the back. The door opened. Luke looked so good. But he didn't react as she expected. He didn't ask her any questions. Instead he told her, "Don't say anything." And he held his hand in front of him as if he could push her objection away if she dared to utter one.

Roxy knew her face must have reflected her surprise. She'd wondered a hundred things while driving back to West Texas, but she never imagined he wouldn't want her to explain what she was doing back in town just ten hours after she'd left him.

He opened the screen door, which was just one of the barriers between them, stepped and then grabbed her hand. He pushed her gently out of the way so he could pull the doors shut behind them. Then he propelled her along to the side of his old pickup.

She opened her mouth to ask him what he thought he was doing but then snapped it shut. He had every right to ask for an explanation. Which she couldn't give him. What *was* she doing back in Red Wing?

"Get in." His deep growl was an order. "I want to show you something."

Roxy obediently climbed into the pickup.

He got into the truck and then he turned toward her. He gave her a grin so wide she could see it in the dark. She grinned in return. It was enough just to be at his side. Roxy settled in his company like she was home.

She looked out the open window into the wide sky as they pulled away from his house, leaving the artificial lights behind. "The stars are incredible, but with no moon there's not enough light for horseback riding or even sight-seeing."

"It's just right for what I have in mind."

Her hand sought his, and feeling content, they drove in the dark silence for another five minutes. Then there was an abrupt bump as the asphalt ran out. Roxy's hand tightened on his. A few minutes later they hit a really rough patch and the truck lurched from side to side. He pulled his hand away to hold on to the steering wheel. Roxy grabbed the door handle. "This road needs some work."

"It's a shortcut."

The truck lurched again. She felt like she was on a

ride at an amusement park without the security of anything to hang on to. "Are you sure this is a good idea?"

"Just hang on. It's going to be worth the ride."

Curious, she strained to see where they were going through the fine dust, which in the headlights looked like thin snow falling.

"How can you see what you're doing?"

"What's to see? The only danger out here is hitting a pothole."

"A pothole? This entire stretch of road is potholes."

"Don't worry. I know this area pretty well."

The truck lurched again and Roxy hissed. The air was thick. She expected she might have to cough up a lung before she cleared all of the dust out of her throat.

"This is like going four-wheeling without the benefit of four-wheel drive. And I'm supposed to feel better because you know the area pretty well? Did anyone ever suggest you could break an axle out here?"

"We're okay."

"*Someone* once told me the temperatures around here sometimes climb to well over a hundred degrees. I've heard a person could die if they get stranded. What happens to them when they're way out in the middle of nowhere?"

"Relax." His deep voice was unaffected by the dust or anything else. "We could walk home before the sun came up. Just roll up your window if the dust's bothering you."

Had he even noticed the sarcasm in her voice?

The truck lurched again and she was thrown against

his long body. She clung to his side, warily watching out for the gearshift. To distract herself she concentrated on her minor grievances. "I don't want to walk home," she complained.

"Then I'll carry you."

Her heart seemed to skip a beat. When you were as tall as she was it was unusual for a man to offer to carry you ten feet, let alone miles through the desert.

She could think of nothing to ease the almost palpable silence between them. Then she spotted a long winding dirt road in the filtered light of their headlights. "You took pity on me and brought us back to the road. A real road."

"It's not a road. It's the riverbed." He eased the truck into the natural groove of the riverbank.

"Are we going swimming?" Roxy's voice reflected her trepidation at the thought of swimming at night with who knew what kind of critters. "Aren't there coyotes out here? I don't want to tangle with a coyote." She shuddered at the thought.

"The coyotes won't bother us, and if we go for a walk we can make enough noise to scare any snakes in the vicinity." He said it in such a matter-of-fact fashion, it didn't register at first.

"Snakes?" she said, perking up. "What kind are indigenous to this area? Besides the obvious—rattlesnakes. I like snakes. I like the really big varieties."

"You're afraid of coyotes, but you like snakes?"

"Yeah, I think snakes are great. I wanted to have one

for a pet but you have to feed it live mice, and I always felt sorry for the mice."

"Woman, you're full of surprises."

His voice sounded admiring. It was almost like he had his arm around her and had given her a warm squeeze. She wondered why he didn't put his arm around her. It would have been the gentlemanly thing to do, and yet he was holding himself almost rigidly away from her. Had she damaged things between them when she'd left town earlier? If so, then why had he rushed her out here?

"What are we doing way out here anyway?"

"There's something I want to show you."

She nodded. But her spirits were sinking. He probably wanted to talk—really talk—and that was the last thing she wanted to do. She couldn't even explain why she'd come back. It had just seemed like the right thing to do, since she'd been so miserable driving away.

Finally he pulled the pickup to a stop. Without any warning he turned off the engine and the night immediately engulfed them. The darkness was so complete Roxy literally couldn't see her hand in front of her face. It wasn't like any darkness she'd experienced before. "Luke?"

His warm hand closed around hers and he pulled her gently toward his door as he stepped out. She felt for the gearshift and navigated around the blasted thing. Then she was at the edge of his seat, dangling half out of the truck.

"Look up."

She looked into the star-studded sky and caught her breath at the wonder of it. "There must be a billion of them." She felt awed.

He chuckled. "Just wait till your eyes have adjusted to the dark. You'll see even more."

"It isn't fair. We don't have this sky in Dallas."

"You have this sky. You just fill it up with light that drowns out the stars. You folks don't see things as clearly in the big city."

She gazed at the sky for what seemed like hours, but was only a few minutes. She couldn't see him but she knew exactly where he was standing. What was going through his mind? What was he going to ask her? What was she going to tell him? What *was* she doing back in Red Wing?

Trying to ease her own tension she rubbed the back of her neck. "I'm getting a kink in my neck. But I'm glad you brought me. I'll remember this forever."

"Come with me." His hand suddenly closing over hers made her jump.

Dumbly she slid down from the pickup and allowed him to lead her around to the back of the truck.

"Stay here while I move a few things around."

Roxy wondered how he could see what he was doing but she stood beside the side of the truck as he'd asked. She found she could follow his actions from the telltale noises coming from the truck bed. The tailgate came down with a rusty protest. As he walked inside the bed of the truck his feet crunched over small pieces of dirt and gravel. She imagined he was wearing his boots.

He cursed under his breath as he fumbled for something. It made her smile. He obviously didn't want her to hear him curse; he was ever the gentleman.

A few small sounds left her with the impression he was trying to make the back a comfortable place to watch the stars, and then he was close to her. "Can you feel the tailgate?"

She nodded and then remembered he couldn't see her. "I've got it." She put her hands on the edge, braced herself, and then swung up onto the back of the pickup. It wasn't easy because for some reason her legs were trembling. So she sat.

He moved around her as if he could easily navigate through the dark. She resented his sure purpose. He brushed by her as he moved deeper into the back of the truck.

"Come closer," he coaxed her. "I want you to see these stars up close and personal. I have to show you what you've been missing in the big city."

"I don't want you to get any ideas. I'm not staying."

"How long?"

"Just tonight."

"Then let's make it memorable."

She sighed. "You wouldn't even touch me in the truck."

"I was afraid we wouldn't make it out of my front yard if I touched you."

Her breathing quickened at his admission. His hand was warm on her arm as he drew her to her feet. "I can see everything just fine if I'm sitting down, and I'm less likely to trip," she protested.

"Please?"

Just a step toward the back of the truck bed and her feet tangled in some thick material. He caught her easily. "Don't worry, I won't let anything happen to you."

She nodded, though she knew he couldn't see her nod. "You always say the most wonderful things in the most matter-of-fact way. It's like you think I'm a precious little thing who needs looking after. It goes to my head." *And my heart.*

He ran his hands up the side of her arms until he touched her hair. He pulled gently, trying to work the thick mess out of the ponytail she'd scraped it into while she was driving.

She reached up to help him, and he drew a sharp breath when her breasts brushed up against his chest. Her hands shook, but in a moment her hair was lying in heavy waves on her shoulders like the residual heat of the day. "I don't like it down when it's hot."

"It's going to get very hot," he promised her as he delicately traced her cheeks, chin and neck with his rough fingers.

"That sounded like a promise." She undid the first button of his shirt. Then she felt her way down the material searching for the next button. The darkness was so thick it was altering everything.

All of her other senses strained to compensate for her lack of sight. The fabric of his shirt felt weighty on her fingertips. His breath grazed her forehead, whispering in her hair. In her head, her heart beat a rhythm of escalating need. Her mouth was dry with dust and anticipation.

He ran his hands lightly over the mound of her breasts, momentarily distracting her from the task at hand. She paused, one hand hovering over his chest. He continued downward as if unmoved. Curious, Roxy ran one hand downward. Did he plan to make love to her?

His reflexes were incredible. He caught the hand before she discovered the evidence she sought.

"No," he protested.

"Why?"

"If you do that I'll just pull you down on this sleeping bag and it will be over in a matter of minutes. I want to explore you. I want to spend eons touching you."

She leaned forward and kissed what felt like the side of his jaw. "Okay," she whispered. Her knees buckled and she grabbed double handfuls of his shirt.

Luke's hands slid down to cup her bottom, momentarily propping her up. It wasn't effective for strengthening her knees, but it did wonderful things to the rest of her.

"I want you naked."

Her heart rate soared.

He unbuttoned her shorts.

She closed her eyes. In her imagination she could see herself, standing in the truck bed, entirely naked bathed only in starlight and his touch.

As he tugged off her shorts, she could barely help

him. It was a gentle tug-of-war with her sandals tangled in the material. Then she was bare from the waist down, and the tiny breeze that dared to flout the desert heat wrapped around her bottom and thighs. The night whispered around them. Goose bumps marched across her skin and she shivered.

His fingers trailed over her. "I know you're not cold."

"Not cold," she repeated.

He knelt and ran his fingers slowly from the top of her feet, then to her calves, finally up the outside of her thighs and over the hills of her buttocks. He paused at her waist.

She choked in a breath. "Stop," she protested in a thin whisper. "I want to feel you, too." She pulled him back to his feet. She found the next button and the next until the shirt lay around his waist, caught in the band of his pants. She couldn't resist running her fingers over his bare chest.

She needed no other evidence of her effect on him than the rapid rise of his chest and the wild beat of his heart.

"It feels like we are totally alone in the world," she murmured.

"In Eden."

She didn't object to his observation. The desert night was just hot enough for them to be comfortable bared to the starlit night. And only Eden had a sky like this one. But she didn't look up. Her fingers explored the bulge of every muscle she'd uncovered.

"More," he told her. His breath was against her ear

until he pulled her shirt up and then over her head. Her hair flopped down and so he smoothed it tenderly.

She felt like screaming. "No." It was a part of the thin breeze. "No, I want..."

"What?" He played with her hair as if he were the mischievous wind.

"I want..." She didn't finish, hoping he would finish it for her.

"Tell me."

She unsnapped his jeans. "I want more of your skin."

She pulled down the tab of his zipper like she was helping him with a striptease.

He wobbled a little.

"What's wrong?" she asked him, though her breath caught in her throat. His arousal was enormous. Her hands shook as she tugged on his pants. He rested one hand on her shoulder as he helped her to take off his jeans and boxers.

She quivered. "This doesn't have to be slow and easy," she whispered. "It can be slow and easy next time."

He pulled her to him and teased her with his mouth and tongue. She deepened the kiss, drinking in his passion. He pulled her up so she nestled against his heat. Rubbing her fingers over his penis she shuddered, kissing him deeper. And when she could breath again she whispered, "Please." It was unashamed begging.

He pushed her hands away. "Not yet, honey," he growled.

He explored her face with his lips and his hands came

around behind her. He unclasped the bra and the back fell open. The wind crept in underneath the loosened cups. His fingers followed. The bra dropped and for a moment she stood alone, suspended against the stars. She looked up just as a star shot across the sky. "Oh."

He pulled her closer and rested his chin on her shoulder, his hand between their bodies, searching for and finding the wet heat between her legs. She rubbed against the pressure she craved, almost whimpering with need.

He grabbed her around the waist; his face buried in her breasts, and then slowly lowered himself to his knees. He laid her down on the thickness of several sleeping bags. She clutched at him, need roaring through her. "Please."

"You're not used to this heat." Abruptly he pulled away from her.

She could hear the hollow thud of plastic. It took a second, but she soon realized he was getting into the cooler where he kept his drinks.

Now he loomed over her, propped up on his elbows, and suddenly he dripped something icy cold against her nipple. Startled, she tried to roll away but he moved closer. Again, he dripped the ice on her heated skin. Then he licked the cold water from her erect nipples. When she gasped with pleasure, he put the ice directly on her flesh. Then he took it away. His mouth was like a furnace compared to the ice.

"Oh, that's so cold."

"Do you like it?"

"Yes," she breathed.

He scooted farther down the length of her body, dripping the water until her belly button became a small icy reservoir. A pool of cold in a landscape of heat.

She shivered and the pool ran over. He licked the water before it hit the sleeping bag. "Be careful."

"Careful? I'm about to go up in smoke here," she gasped.

"Then I'll have to keep trying to cool you off."

The contrast was so sensual she found herself panting, gasping for breath with each icy rivulet he spilled over her flesh.

The water drizzled down her thighs and he chased the chilly drops with his tongue. She lifted her hips, unable to remain still while he tormented her, and the puddle became an icy path from her belly button to between her legs. She shuddered. He raised up and dried her with his tongue.

Then he got a new piece of ice while she lay panting with anticipation. This time the dripping ice puddled in the hollows of her hips. For a moment she lay shuddering. Then he lapped the already warm liquid with long hot strokes.

Another piece of ice came out of the cooler. This time the icy water ran directly over the hot wet flesh between her legs. She almost screamed. She knew she was going to come without him and yet she wanted to hold on, to share all she could with him, when he finally claimed her.

The ice melted between her legs. His mouth lovingly followed every drip.

His tongue on her sensitive folds was hot, his fingers icy as they pushed rhythmically, deeper and deeper inside of her.

"You like that?" he taunted her. "I can do this all night long. I'm going to get you so hot you'll beg me to put the ice inside you."

"Come here!" She pulled him up, face-to-face. His body stuck to hers with the moisture between them. She reached between to stroke the silky length of his penis. He was so hot. "Luke, I want you. I want you, please."

He muttered something, kissed her ruthlessly, and then he grabbed a package from under the edge of the sleeping bag. In a moment he had the condom on, and then he gave her his glorious weight. He filled her with heat, stretching, and thrusting into her until the desert wasn't just all around her. The heat was inside her, building, until she took off to join the icy dance of the stars.

11

MICK FOSSER SAW THE LIGHT. It was just as Roxy had described on the phone. A really ugly green light lending the bleak landscape a Martian cast over a mom-and-pop type motel. He pulled his black Mustang into the parking lot.

For a moment he stretched his legs, walking back and forth in the parking lot. He pulled a cigarette out of his pocket and lit it. There was still a lot of heat in the air, even at full dark. He checked his watch. Ten o'clock. *And I'm not drinking.* He shook his head, unsure why he'd come.

But he knew. His brother wasn't getting out of the hospital for a few more days. Joey's liver wasn't recovering as quickly as they'd like. Lots of doctor mumbo jumbo. Even Joey looked scared.

I'm scared.

He put his hands in his pockets. He wasn't really scared. He just needed a distraction and the thought of going back to Roxy's museum of a house didn't sit well. He just needed to talk to Roxy, in person. Needed to tell her what was going down, and have her tell him in plain English that his brother was going to be all right.

I'm not scared.

He hurried inside the motel.

"Hello, young fellow," said the old guy behind the counter.

"Hello, yourself. You got any rooms?"

"Smoking or nonsmoking?"

Mick was pretty sure there were rooms available. It was Sunday, and there had only been three other cars outside. He got the impression the man asked the question out of habit.

I got a habit. He put out the cigarette in the ashtray on the counter.

"Smoking," he told the old man.

"Sure. Got a smoking single for you. No problem." The man placed a card on the counter. "Just fill out this registration form for me, and I'll get you a key. Will you be paying with cash or a credit card?"

As Mick pulled his Visa card out of his wallet he asked, "Have you got a Roxanne Adams registered? She's a friend of mine from Dallas and I'm looking for her."

The old man looked him over as he took the credit card. "Guess there's no harm in telling you. She's checked out, already. You missed her, boy."

Mick's spirits sank. So did any hope of him getting through the night without a few...beers. He'd stick to beer. He pushed his hair off of his forehead. "Did she say where she was going?"

"She picked up her little car and headed back to Dallas, last I heard."

Mick nodded. "Well, I'm glad I took the scenic tour

on the way up. That way I won't feel I missed anything when I turn around tomorrow and go back home."

The old man laughed. "The scenic tour? Huh, that's a good one. You don't see anything around here but dirt and cactus.

Despite his joke, Mick didn't feel any better, though he tried to smile.

"I just rang you up for one night. You change your mind, you just let me know." The old man handed him the key.

Mick took it and went out to his car. He knew where to go. All small towns were alike. The bar would be just outside town. Right now, its neon would be a lot more welcoming than the motel's.

He drove.

The neon wasn't very far away. He turned off the road into a parking lot filled with dust and old pickups. He activated his alarm as he walked toward the door. The dust swirled up around him and just for a moment he looked up into a sky loaded with stars. When was the last time he'd looked up at the stars?

When he opened the door to the bar, country music blasted past him. He grinned. He preferred heavy metal, but it all sounded the same after he had enough to drink. He made his way to the bar, aware of the stares he was collecting. He shrugged to himself. What did it matter if the local yokels stared? No one here knew him. He could wallow in despair if he wanted to. Just spend this one night in a strange town to let off some steam. Roxy had found something here. He could hear it in her voice. What would he find?

"What'll it be, mister?" The bartender was a gray-haired woman whose face was stretched so tightly by her enormous weight she didn't have a single wrinkle.

"A beer and a shot of JD."

As she waited for the golden beer to fill up his mug, she looked over, studying him curiously. "We don't get many visitors. Where are you from?"

"Dallas. I'm looking for a friend of mine. Maybe you've seen her in here? Her name is Roxanne Adams. She's hard to miss. A tall redhead."

"She ain't been in here. I heard she was at The Golden Pan for a spell."

He nodded. So Roxy had avoided the bar. He pushed the shot a little ways away from him and took a sip of the beer.

A woman sat down on the bar stool beside him. He turned and smiled at the petite blonde. "Can I buy you a drink?" he offered.

"I would love a drink. I'll have a beer, Jane," she told the bartender.

He drained the beer and signaled to the bartender for another. Then he faced the blonde, reminding himself he needed to be cool. He shouldn't go dumping all his problems on her just because she was here and he was feeling like a fool. She'd run for the hills. He cleared his throat. "Hi. My name's Mick Fosser. I'm from Dallas."

"I'm Carla Rae Sweeny and I've lived here all my life. What are you doing in Red Wing?"

For a moment the thought of Roxy's expectations made him hesitate. *What am I doing here? I wish I knew.*

But the shot sat at his elbow untouched.

When that second beer arrived he gratefully wrapped his hands around the cool handle of the mug. *It's only beer. So far I'm sticking to the beer like a good boy.* "I'm just passing through."

She took a sip of her beer. She was dressed in a denim dress that outlined all of her slender curves. "I thought I heard you tell Jane you were looking for a friend of yours."

He shrugged. "She wouldn't be here. She doesn't drink anymore. I think she had some car trouble out here but the man at the motel said she left yesterday."

"She doesn't drink *anymore?* What's her name? Roxanne?"

"Yeah, she's a friend of mine from way back."

"A girlfriend?" Carla put her hand next to his on the scarred bar. Her long nails traced a path just shy of his hand.

"No, not that sort of friend."

"Oh." She looked disappointed and her hand fell away from his.

"She's been a friend of mine for years. She used to work in my bar and then she helped my brother get into AA."

Shut up, man, when did you get so pathetic?

He buried his face in the beer so he wouldn't say any more. And he signaled for another.

Carla faced him. "You own a bar? What's it like?"

"It's a rough place. Not anywhere a lady like you would be interested in going. It's also for sale. I'm looking for a change."

She raised an eyebrow. "A man like you?"

He knew what she saw. A man with a day's growth of beard that couldn't quite hide the scar on his chin from a fight in his bar. Her sharp eyes would have noticed the red clouding his blue eyes, and the gray threading his black hair. But he was slim, more rangy than muscular, but fit enough at thirty to go a couple of rounds with a rowdy customer if it came down to it. "Even a man like me."

"I know your friend," she said abruptly.

He smiled. "Isn't she great?"

Carla fiddled with her napkin. "How exactly did she get your brother into AA?"

"She got him into her group. It took a lot of convincing but she'd been pestering him forever."

"She drinks? You mean that she's got a drinking problem?" Carla's voice rose several notches.

"She doesn't anymore. Not for a long time."

"You sound proud of her." Carla kinda wilted into the bar.

"I am. She went through a lot of shit."

"How hard can it be? She's obviously rich. I saw her car. I told Luke that she'd drive her little car right over his heart. And I was right, damn it. I'm right," she sniffed. Her big blue eyes welled up with tears.

Mick put his hands up. "Please don't cry. Please." Women's tears always made him feel helpless. He handed her a cocktail napkin, hoping she'd quit the waterworks.

"Thanks," she sniffled into it.

He reached out and grasped her hand. "Don't cry."

She tried to smile, but it didn't reach her glistening eyes.

He started talking as fast as he could to cut the flow of tears. "I came to Red Wing to see Roxy. My brother's been sick and she knows what this is like. She understands family trouble and she's been to rock bottom."

He rubbed his hand along the bar. Then he glanced at the untouched shot on the bar. He reached for the fresh beer Jane slid to him. *I am not at rock bottom.*

"Trouble? Well, I'm not surprised." Again her voice rose above the din around them. Heads turned in their direction.

He shook his head. "Yeah, being wealthy doesn't insulate you from trouble. You can be brought as low as any bum on the street. She was so drunk at times she didn't know where she was and she didn't care. It's ironic, girl like that living on the streets. See how it was? The money didn't help her. How could it? But we helped her and then she helped us—I mean, she helped my brother." It felt good to talk and it seemed Carla needed to confide in someone almost as much as he did.

Carla looked around the room.

"Expecting a boyfriend?" Mick asked, and then he took a deep drink of his beer. He didn't want to have to deck an angry boyfriend.

Carla shook her head. "Go on. Tell me more about Roxy."

"I just thought I'd check on her. She's been here longer than she expected."

"You must be pretty good friends."

"We go way back."

"Well, your friend, Roxy sure fixed up my life," Carla said bitterly. "I thought Luke kept putting off our long-term plans because he wasn't ready to settle down. I was patient because I trusted him."

Mick ran a hand through his hair. "Luke? Isn't that the name of the sheriff who rescued her from the side of the road?"

"Yeah. Seems your heroine isn't so noble after all, given she didn't think about seducing my man."

"He told you Roxy seduced him?"

"Neither one of them told me. The entire town saw his pickup outside of the diner and heard the jukebox going after hours. What am I supposed to think they were doing?" Her voice rose again.

Mick looked around the bar. The bartender gave him a tight smile, then turned away. He shook his head and eyed Carla thoughtfully. "Unless I miss my guess, you made sure everyone in here caught every word you and I've said about Roxy tonight. Why would you do that?"

Carla nodded. "You're quick enough." She paused and then her face changed, suddenly looking weary and defeated. "I don't know what I'm doing. Luke's gonna be in hot water once everyone knows what kinda girl he's got himself hooked up with."

Mick eyed the shot. "I didn't come here to hurt one of my best friends. She's a good person." *Better than me.*

Carla shook her head. "Can you see her as the wife of the sheriff of a small town? Can you see her buried in Red Wing?"

He shrugged. He didn't know. Roxy already lived between worlds, her dad's mansion, the run-down high school where she worked, and then her condo, which was nothing fancy. It seemed she could make herself at home anywhere, but at the moment, he was more interested in Carla. "I can understand why you're angry at Roxy. But what I don't understand is why a pretty lady like you would want to be buried here and tied to a man who doesn't love her?"

She sighed. "I love this little town. I love the familiar places. I guess I knew Luke and I weren't really in love. Not the earth shakin' kind, anyway. I think I just wanted the best man in town to be the father of my kids."

Mick lifted her pretty hand from on top of the bar and held it. "It's no sin, you know, being lonely."

She looked up into his face. Her eyes were such a deep, beautiful blue. "How'd you know I've been lonely?"

He thought he could drown in those eyes, "I guess I'm familiar with the symptoms."

ROXY WOKE UP to a mosquito buzzing around her nose. While swatting it she discovered she was lying naked on top of a mound of sleeping bags in the bed of Luke's truck.

It had to be near morning, she mused. The desert air was actually cool. The budding of her naked breasts made her deliciously aware of her femininity. Luke had done this for her. He'd given her back the piece of herself she'd squandered on a filthy man in an alcoholic stupor. She sent a word of thanks to the creator of those dazzling stars and then attempted to go back to sleep.

But sleep eluded her. She felt so alive. Revitalized. Perhaps, she didn't need to fear she'd slip into the habit of her old life. She lay with her eyes closed and spun dreams of a future with a house and children on the edge of a desert.

Dreams as nebulous as the cool air around her.

Luke rolled over and she opened her eyes. She noticed it at once: the stars were going out, one by one. The illumination of the rising sun extinguished them. Dread settled in the pit of her stomach.

You're being silly. Sunrises are beginnings. But the sense of dread didn't fade.

"Good morning." His morning voice was deep and sexy. It curled around her like the scent of fine coffee.

If I had to lose him then I want to enjoy today.

But she'd said that yesterday, and the day before and so on. So far it hadn't made things any easier. Still, the dread mixed with anticipation. Anticipation won. Roxy enjoyed the flush of awakening desire.

"What are you thinking about?" He looked adorably vulnerable with his hair standing on end.

She wasn't ready to tell him what was really on her mind. He'd think she was the most wanton woman in the world. "Coffee," she said hurriedly. "I'm thinking about coffee." She tugged the corner of a sleeping bag over her naked lap.

He sat up. "I've got some drinks in the cooler."

She could feel her face go scarlet at the mention of the cooler. The warmth of her flush reminded her of heated flesh and the cool release of ice. She ignored the urge to cover her breasts with her arms. Let him look—maybe he would be inspired to take up where they'd left off last night.

"Sure, I'd like something to drink." Despite her attempt to look unaffected by either her nudity or her desire, her voice sounded strangled.

He pulled the cooler from the side where it had been nestled against the wheel well. He opened it and pulled out a dripping Dr. Pepper. As the water ran down the maroon can and then over his naked wrist, she imagined licking the water off him, and blushed harder.

"They're not cold." He sounded almost mournful.

She took the can he offered. It was almost warm. "How did the ice stay so long last night? You had the cooler in my car, and then in the back of your truck. The ice should have been melted. I'd been gone all day."

"You mean the ice I used on you?"

She made an issue of placing the can carefully in the cradle of her lap. She hunched in on herself, not sure if she could look him in the eyes. "Yes."

He put his fingers under her chin. "I like it when

you're shy," he told her. "I also like it when you're demanding. You nearly killed me last night."

She pushed his hand away. "Why did you have fresh ice in the cooler? You didn't know I was coming back."

"Are you jealous?"

"Don't be ridiculous. You can have Carla. I *want* you to have Carla. The town loves Carla." She crossed her arms over her breasts.

He scratched his head. "Fine. I must have planned on bringing Carla out here and using the ice on her, but then you showed up, saving me a trip to town."

Still covering herself, she curled her fingers into her palms lest she give in to the desire to hurt him, badly.

"Don't pout." He rubbed his shoulder up against hers like a cat. Only he was naked, and she couldn't help but notice he was aroused.

"I put the cooler in the car about two minutes before you pulled up. I was going to come out here and think. I was going to lie on the sleeping bags, drink Dr. Pepper, and think about you." He nudged her with his shoulder. "I have to tell you you look positively dangerous when you're jealous. And it's my job to avert acts of violence," he said in a mock official tone.

"I'm not jealous," she protested halfheartedly. But Roxy felt the tension drip away like the water off a Dr. Pepper. She dropped her arms. She reached for the soda and then popped the tab. The sweet scent bubbled up. She looked at him boldly. Considering. "You like this stuff so much, maybe I'll just pour a little on you this morning." She could imagine a small puddle of the sweet liquid pooled on his concave stomach. She'd lap it up until he begged her to venture lower.

He looked intrigued. "The mosquitoes will probably come after us in droves," he said as if they were discussing the sunrise or the weather.

She couldn't help but notice how eager he was. Still, she pretended nonchalance. "If big, bad Farmer John's worried about mosquitoes, I understand." She scratched her nose and reached down to shove the corner of the sleeping bag from her lap. "I tangled with a ferocious one earlier."

"I suppose my professional reputation would be in shreds if I let a few mosquitoes keep me from using 'my weapon.'"

She giggled. "I think you can handle this situation. Then again if your gun misfires, it won't be worth getting bitten."

"I'll show you," he growled. "I'm going to make you beg."

"We'll see who'll be begging."

He stood up, stretching. "Just give me a minute to check in. I'll use the radio in the truck. After you've had your way with the Dr. Pepper, we can visit the salt pond for a bath. I'll scrub your back and your front and..."

She bit back a groan of frustration as he climbed out of the truck bed and then went around to the cab. "You don't know what you're missing," she told him.

He paused, one hand on the door handle. "Don't worry, I'm not going to miss any of your sweet skin."

He gave her a lascivious once-over and then ducked inside the truck.

A moment later, she heard a loud curse from the cab. Then he stuck his head out the door. "I'm sorry, darlin'. We've got some trouble this morning. We've spoken of the devil, and she's struck. It seems Carla met up with your friend Mick last night and ended up taking him home with her."

12

THEY HAD ALMOST REACHED town when Luke pulled off the main road into a deserted parking lot with a decaying pawn shop. He wanted to talk to Roxy alone. He put the truck in Park and then turned to her.

Her body language was defensive. He missed the open, sexy woman he'd been with this morning, but that Roxy had slipped away. "We need to talk."

"We need to go get Mick. What's he doing with Carla? And why would she call the dispatcher to tell you about him? I don't trust Carla," she muttered.

"Now, you've got the wrong idea about Carla. She's a real nice woman. Just like you when you're not jealous as a hellcat."

She blushed. She *had* been ready to pound on him if he hadn't come up with such a good excuse for having fresh ice in the cooler. "Okay, I'm willing to give her the benefit of the doubt before I throw her down and sit on her," she told him reluctantly.

"That's my girl. Maybe I should be jealous of Mick."

"Mick?" She shook her head. "No. He's been like a brother to me."

He nodded. The look in his eyes reached right into

her heart. "Please, Roxy, tell me what you've been hiding from me. Tell me about Mick."

"What do you want to know? A friend of mine came to see me. That's all."

He just looked at her.

She reached up to drag her hair in front of her face. "I live in Dallas and I want to go back. Is it a crime? Can't you imagine a life that doesn't include really extreme temperatures, fires, dust storms and a town full of gossips?"

"It has its benefits," he told her gravely. "I thought you were coming to understand the beauty of this place. I know I've loved seeing it through your eyes."

"Let's just go." Roxy ruthlessly cut off the part of herself whispering that she needed to touch him.

He started the old truck and they moved out of the parking lot. They quickly reached a little white house with a picket fence and a lush flower bed. Because it was still cool, the shaded porch looked almost welcoming.

"She's got a lot of flowers."

"Yeah, around here most people don't bother but Carla's a nurturer."

The door opened and Mick walked out onto the porch. Roxy slipped out of the pickup and then ran up to give him a hug. "Mick, how are you? I was so worried."

He gave her a squeeze but his smile didn't quite reach his eyes. "I'm glad to see you. The man at the motel told me you'd left town."

"I did, but I came back, but...oh, it's a long story." She turned to see if Luke had followed her. Both Carla and Luke stood close by on the porch. "I'll tell you later. For now Luke and I are going to take you to the motel and we can catch up. Just the two of us. How's Joey?"

"Joey's fine. We just spoke to him on the phone," Carla said. She looked fresh and pretty dressed in shorts and a pink shirt, just like one of her flowers.

Roxy felt like a slob in her wrinkled shorts and top. "What did you say?" She rubbed her palms on her shorts.

"I said we talked to Joey this morning. His liver functions are almost normal and he's feeling better. Mick says the doctors are more optimistic today than they were yesterday."

Roxy felt as if all the air had been let out of her. She couldn't seem to control the fear and anger running through her. She looked at Mick. "What did you tell her?"

Mick hung his head. "I'm afraid I was indiscreet last night in the bar."

Hysteria threatened to overwhelm Roxy. She felt her knees go weak. "What? Did you tell the whole town?"

"It's my fault," Carla said.

Roxy kept her gaze on Mick. How could he betray her?

Luke grabbed her arm. "Don't do this. Don't get all riled up. It's bad for your blood sugar and you'll end up in the clinic. Just take a deep breath. I'm sure they're exaggerating."

Roxy leaned on Luke. She absorbed his warmth, his strength, and then took a deep breath.

"We're not exaggerating. Mick was sitting at the bar and he said everything in front of Jane." Carla looked first at Luke, and then, with real sympathy in her eyes, at Roxy. "I'm sorry, Roxy. I wanted everyone to know you weren't good enough for him, so I encouraged Mick to talk about you in front of Jane and everyone. I know it was wrong. I'm really sorry for my part in this."

"This is unbelievable." Roxy pulled away from Luke, wrapping her arms around herself. *I'm going to lose him now.*

She walked away from them and sat down on the front stoop as if her legs had lost their strength.

Luke settled down beside her. She could hear the soft thud of the door closing behind them. "Roxy, please, be honest with me. I think I've earned some honesty from you."

A tear slipped down her face. "You don't want to know about me."

His dark eyes implored her. "Trust me."

She shook her head. She wiped her eyes and tried a shaky smile. "We made some really nice memories."

He reached toward where his badge would have been if he hadn't been wearing the jeans and simple T-shirt from last night. She knew he was going to say something plain and touching, something with the power to change her mind.

She bit the inside of her lip, grateful for the steadying pain. She continued on before he could protest. "This town loves you. They'll forgive this little indiscretion before the next election. Carla will forgive you, and everything will be back to normal in Red Wing. That's all that's important."

"Roxy got my brother into AA," Mick said, from behind them. When they turned to look at him he shrugged and held up two mugs. "Carla thought you might like some coffee."

"Haven't you done enough damage?" Roxy said with a shake of her head.

Mick set the coffee between them on the porch. Then he straightened and wiped his hands over his face. He looked directly at Luke. "They both tried to get me to dry out. I wasn't strong enough but Joey was, and for six months he did it, but he fell off the wagon and then he tried to kill himself. It sucked me down." He shrugged. "Made me realize stuff. I needed to talk to Roxy."

Roxy took a deep breath. "I'm so sorry I wasn't there for you, Mick. I should have come home right away."

Mick just shook his head. "You should have done exactly what you did." He looked at the door, almost longingly. "I'm going to go help Carla with breakfast." He escaped as fast as he could.

Roxy lowered her head to her knees.

"Do you think I'm going to hold AA against you?" Luke's voice was an intrusion from a world that didn't include people like her and Mick.

At this moment she bitterly resented him. She didn't

even look up. "Luke, you couldn't possibly understand my life and I can't explain it."

"What can't I understand? You've made an awful lot of assumptions about me."

Righteous anger gave her the strength to face him. "I was always honest with you. I didn't intend to do anything but have a holiday. As for assumptions, you were the one who tapped on my window with a whole lot of assumptions."

"I did make assumptions. Then you went and proved them all wrong. It was exactly what I needed in order to take a good hard look at where my life was going. I owe you."

Roxy rubbed her arms. "All of your original assumptions were correct. Your instincts were right. I'm bad news. I always have been. I didn't tell you because I knew we wouldn't be together for more than a few days."

"What if I want more than just a few days?"

"It's not possible. I'm not someone you could admire. I'm not a Carla, darling of the town. Just ask anyone. By now everyone in this town knows my sordid past."

"Everyone except me. Tell me what you're hiding. You don't have to be alone."

There was so much compassion in his face, almost enough to undo her intentions. She dug her fingernails into her arm so she wouldn't give in and she wouldn't cry. *I will not be selfish.* It echoed in her mind.

"Please tell me about Joey."

Was Luke jealous? Did he think there was anyone

else in the world she was willing to make this sacrifice for? Didn't he know how hard it was going to be to walk away from her Farmer John?

"He was my friend and Mick's brother. He hurt himself. It just proved all my confidence in being sober was based on *nothing*. I'm still weak. I'll always be just waiting to slip back into old habits."

"What happened exactly?"

He sounded so much like a lawman trying to get to the bottom of things she almost smiled through her heartbreak. "Joey's attempt brought it all back—my brother's overdose, finding his body. I'm like him. Like them. Addicted. Weak. Out of control."

"I want you, Roxy. I have almost from the moment I laid eyes on you. I don't think you're weak. You're strong."

Everything he felt for her was there in his voice and Roxy felt it. Her eyes teared up. She couldn't do this. Time to get rid of Luke once and for all.

"I was a drunk, Luke. There are bums on the street with more integrity than I had. I've been so low. Everything Carla said about me was right."

"You're wrong. You obviously don't drink anymore."

"Do you think it will matter to the voters in Red Wing? They'll never reelect you. Will you sell cars for a woman who isn't worth it? A woman who might not be strong enough to stay sober? Will you throw your life away?"

"You're worth it."

Damn him. He had no right to reach in and squeeze her heart. "Don't."

"Don't what?"

"Don't pretend that this job is not a part of who you are. Even when you're in civilian clothing you reach for your badge. You worry about your town. The last thing you deserve is to lose this town."

He took her hands. "I won't lose you."

"You never had me. Luke, I have a record. I was a drunk and even...a slut. You are too good to understand how low I've been. I don't want to taint you with my mistakes. I never meant for this to happen. I just thought I could have some nice memories to take home with me. I'm so sorry I've hurt you." She wiped a tear from her eye.

"You don't trust me to love you no matter who you are. Roxy, I love you."

She couldn't cry. The pain was too deep for tears. "You *can't* love me. You don't even know who I am."

He shook his head. "I'm sorry you don't believe in me. But I want you. It doesn't matter who you were in the past."

"And when they won't reelect you? The entire town will know my history in a few hours." Just in case he wouldn't think about himself she added, "And I'm not sure I can handle the stress of everyone in your town staring and talking about me. I'd end up drinking or diabetic."

When he opened his mouth to speak, she rushed on. "You're so good. It would likely kill you if I reverted to my true self. Believe me, this is for the best. I almost gave in to temptation when Joey nearly died. I'm not ready for a normal life yet, even if I was given the chance for one."

He put his hand on her shoulder. "I don't give a damn about what this town thinks of you. But I won't fight you. Not if it will affect your health. Not this way. If you think the past matters then you're the one who doesn't know me very well. I almost settled for less when I was with Carla. I'm not making that mistake again."

She nodded. She always knew he would say goodbye to her once he knew everything. It was inevitable. She understood, he was trying to let her down easy. It was better this way. They could both still salvage their pride.

She resisted the urge to fall to her knees and beg him to convince her to stay.

"I need to borrow the keys to your pickup. I'll leave them on the table at the house. Carla can run you home after you eat breakfast. Tell Mick I'll see him at home."

She sniffed, "He seems to have found something here."

"And you haven't?"

"I can't. I just can't." Bowing her head, she felt him place the keys in her palm, and she gripped them tightly.

"Whatever you need, Roxy. I don't want you to get sick. But I have no..."

She didn't hear the rest as she stumbled from the

stoop. "Goodbye, Luke." It came out a whisper in between sobs as she ran toward the truck.

She peeled out of the driveway. After driving mindlessly for several minutes she stopped the truck. She collapsed on the old seat.

Breathe, she told herself. *Don't think. Just breathe in and then out.* It was difficult. She'd lost Luke. She'd lost the whole world.

13

AT THE SOUND OF THE BELL, Roxy walked across the room to open the door, sure it was either Mick or her father. They'd been hovering over her since she'd got home. In fact Joey had just called and demanded she visit him, again.

The three of them were becoming a real nuisance.

Resolutely she opened the door to her apartment in a major state of dishevelment—maybe they'd leave her alone if she wasn't dressed to go anywhere. She blinked her swollen eyes at the young man on her porch. It wasn't her father. It was Junior.

No, it can't be Junior. She looked again. It was surely Junior, and the melancholy guardian of the sheriff was smiling.

"What the heck are you doing here?" she demanded, slapping a hand over the large rip in the front of her shorts. "Why aren't you in Red Wing where you belong?"

His smile faded. "Why would you assume I belong in Red Wing? I told you I go to college during the school year."

"Okay, Junior, I reiterate, what are you doing on my doorstep?"

"Boy, you sound like a teacher, but this doesn't look like the digs of the woman who owns a screaming yellow Porsche. That reminds me, you promised to let me drive your car."

Roxy shook her head. "Sorry, this isn't a good time."

He shrugged. "The truth is I came to see if you're missing Luke. I figured you'd forget him right away. I thought you'd have a bunch of boyfriends to keep you company. But you look like hell."

She straightened up. "I don't look like hell."

"So you miss Luke? Even though he ain't ever going to have any money or anything?"

"I don't miss him."

Junior took a deep breath. He looked around as if he was reluctant to tell her something. "Luke might be missing you. He mopes around. No one likes him anymore because all he does is growl at them."

She grabbed the doorjamb in a death grip. *I won't listen to him. All I have to do is take a step back, grab the door, and shut it in his face.* "I'm sorry but I have things to do."

Junior nodded. "Sure," he said with a casual nod. "A rich girl like you has to go to the country club for the evening. Poor, old small-town guy like Luke wouldn't have a chance with a woman like you."

"Luke's not old!"

"Lately, he acts like he's a hundred. I can see why you cut out."

She wasn't sure if his bravado was real or manufactured. "What's your major? Drama?" she asked, leveling a knowing look at him.

Unfazed, he answered, "No, it's agriculture. Look, I just stopped to clue you in that Luke's turned into a grumpy old man, and as much as I hate to admit it, he was more fun when he was chasing you around like a teenager, even if he was embarrassing himself in front of the whole county."

She remembered the way Luke had looked when they were handing out sandwiches after the fire. He'd even saluted her with his glass of tea. She remembered them standing drenched in starlight and desire.

A different expression crept across her face. It was as if her muscles hardly remembered how to complete even a hint of a smile after weeks of misery.

But reality stole the smile.

"You were right about what you said earlier. Luke isn't good enough for me. We live in two different worlds."

Junior pushed past her and barged into her apartment. He gestured around. "Yeah, I can tell from your place, money means everything to you. This couch, it looks like an example of a fine antique. Early garage sale, isn't it?"

She resisted the urge to protest his criticism of her ancient, comfortable love seat.

"And this oak table. I'll bet you can't get one at any store in town. It's so special."

Roxy didn't correct him although the oak table had cost one month of her teacher's paycheck. He was mistaking a lack of clutter for a lack of quality, except for the old love seat, which had been David's favorite.

"You rich folk have standards," he continued. "You've got to angle for the big fish."

Roxy just nodded. Let him rant. He'd leave soon.

"I thought you felt something for Luke." His tone was accusing as hell.

Her hands tightened on the doorknob. She wanted to throttle him. "Don't think. Just go away. What gives you the right to decide my fling in Red Wing was true love?"

"I guess I'm pretty naive."

Roxy looked at the tiles in her front entrance hall. "True love doesn't exist. Some people have chemistry between them, but it's short-lived. It's better if two people live the same sort of life and call it love."

He perched on the top of her couch. "I saw how you looked at each other when we took the sandwiches out to the fire. You're making a mistake and making him miserable."

"How dare you come into my house to tell me Luke's unhappiness is somehow my fault!" She slammed the door. Too bad he was on the wrong side of it.

"You want him to go back to Carla? Well, you took care of Carla, too. She's in Dallas, too. She's visiting Mick."

"Mick?" *Damn him for not telling her!*

"Yeah, you're missing out on all the news. Did you know Lisa had a nine-pounder?"

Despite her guilt, Roxy lied. "I didn't talk to Lisa. What do I care if she had the baby?"

"I don't believe you," he told her. "You're not very good at lying."

Roxy almost stamped her feet in frustration. "Okay. I sent a baby gift. I sent the gift and she wrote to tell me how no one listened to the gossip Carla was spreading around. She told me to come back to Red Wing because Luke wouldn't even eat supper at the restaurant anymore, he was starting to look like a scarecrow and no one could get a civil word out of him."

It was painful to talk about him, to speak his name. To know he was hurting when she'd known all along their fling couldn't be more than temporary.

It was her fault. Eventually she always failed. She sagged into her love seat.

"Lisa's exaggerating." He shrugged, obviously torn.

Junior's loyalty was touching. He was a better friend to Luke than she'd ever been. "Junior, go away. You can't possibly understand what's going on between Luke and me. You're too young and inexperienced."

He shook his head. "You and Luke had something special. I guess I'm just naive enough to believe you should go for it."

"It was a fling." She pulled a piece of hair over her shoulder to run it against her cheek.

"Then why did you dance at the restaurant? Why did you stay out all night at the riverbed? That doesn't sound like a night at the Ritz." He lowered his head as if embarrassed.

She threw up her hand in frustration. "Does everyone know our business? Nothing is sacred in Red Wing.

See, this is why our relationship could never work. There are too many people in Red Wing who would be watching our every move. It's like the paparazzi or something."

Junior walked around the couch and this time he sat down on the top of her oak coffee table as if he owned it. "First thing, yes, everyone in Red Wing knows everyone else's warts. It's part of living in a small community."

Roxy curled her arms around herself. "I happen to have more warts than usual, and I don't want them examined by the locals."

Junior ignored her objection. "Secondly, that means everyone knows how hard Luke fell for you."

Suddenly Roxy couldn't breathe. She shook her head.

"Thirdly, there are actually a few benefits to having a whole town looking out for you."

Roxy sat up. "Hah! I don't believe it for a moment. The good people of Red Wing can't wait to stab you in the back the minute you turn around—even if you're the sheriff. And Luke would be the one bleeding. You can't possibly understand."

For the first time he faced her without bravado.

"I understand," he told her. "I'm an alcoholic, too."

He knew everything. Roxy flung herself into the cushions of the love seat, burrowing deeply for comfort.

"Did you hear me?" he insisted.

"Yeah." She raised her head enough to respond to him, because she couldn't ignore what he'd had the courage to say. "I heard you say you're an alcoholic and

I admire you for admitting it to me. Are you getting help?"

"I'm fine. I only told you so you'd understand Luke, and Red Wing." He looked as if he'd rather be anywhere but in her apartment. His valiancy tore at her heart.

"My dad beat me on a regular basis so I paid him back by stealing his liquor and getting into trouble." He gave her a try at a smile. "It wasn't long before I was spending the entire day liquored up. I broke the law and Luke was waiting there to pick up the pieces."

Roxy sniffed, "He would."

Junior nodded. "He got me into an AA program and he drove me to the meetings two hours away. He found me a place to stay and kicked my butt if my grades dropped."

"I'm glad it has a happy ending."

"I tried to hurt him all the time. Every time I struck out at him he told me he was disappointed in me, but he never gave up. Pretty soon I realized he would never get out of my way so I'd better cooperate. I even threw up on him once when he came to collect me from a party."

"You were a kid. Of course he helped you."

He shook his head. "You're stubborn."

"I am not." Roxy sought to evade the web he was weaving around her. "What does this have to do with me, anyway?"

"He loves you. The whole town's grieving for the man who loves you. You have to come back."

"I'd be as welcome as the plague."

"Some people won't accept you. Some people will. But everyone will be glad to have their sheriff back."

Roxy leaped out of her chair. "So I should allow them to feel sorry for me just so Luke gets reelected? Is that why you're really here? To see that your hero keeps his job as sheriff?"

Junior's expression hardened as he stood up. "I thought you were trying to protect Luke by staying away. I thought it meant you really cared about him. I can see I was wrong. The only one you've been trying to protect is yourself." He walked toward the door.

"Junior, you're not being fair!" she wailed.

He looked at her over his shoulder. "How many times have you said that? When are you going to stop whining and grab on to your life? You've paid your debt. There's a place in West Texas where you can have a decent life. Not always an easy life, but a future with a good man."

He opened the door and then walked out with so little fanfare Roxy felt deflated. How could he have seen so much? He was just a kid who didn't know anything. She was the adult. *I'm the adult, damn it!* She buried her face in the old couch and had a good cry. When she finally got up, Junior's challenge still rang in her ears. Her soul ached. She wanted Luke. She wanted a drink. If she couldn't have one, perhaps she needed to have the other.

Anything to dull this pain.

THE BAR SMELLED THE SAME. A hundred memories crowded her like friends, coaxing her from the door-way, whispering of escape. Soon, her need for Luke would be lost in an alcoholic haze, sweet oblivion from pain and guilt.

Luke was unhappy.

Tough. He'll only be more unhappy without his job.

She ached to lay her troubles at this door. She was tired of hurting, tired of fighting herself. Just one drink. Just a few moments to set down her weary load.

And I'll still be in control. I know I can have one beer and relax without losing it. Mick does it.

Just one drink. It wouldn't turn into a drunken binge unless she chose it.

I was strong enough to leave Luke behind—for his own good. So, I'm strong enough to handle one drink.

The floor was sticky and the bar crowded with peo-ple. They looked past her—they didn't want to see each other too closely, unless it led to another kind of escape, sex without care, lust without pain. For a moment she seemed to catch the smell of old vomit.

What are you doing?

She was just visiting. She hadn't come here to stay. She was just having a beer, one beer. She couldn't han-dle this situation straight. She couldn't handle feeling torn apart because all she wanted to do was be with Luke. Why had her life become a series of dangerous addictions?

You're weak and worthless, a part of her argued.

A beer was safer than going back to Luke.

This is the coward's way out, her conscience accused.

Okay, so she was a coward.

She stopped at the wide wooden bar. The bartender filled several mugs before he made eye contact with her. "What will it be?" he asked.

Her knees were weak. She grabbed on to the bar with both hands lest she slide into the dark place in her soul. Hadn't the booze always kept her from looking too deeply into the well of her life? Hadn't she always been afraid the depth of her soul was full of shadows? How many times had she been told by a frustrated caregiver that she was rotten, not worth loving? Hadn't her mother chosen pills over her own children?

"I'll have a draft beer."

The bartender looked at her carefully.

She figured he was wondering how much she'd already had, and if she were likely to cause him trouble. She couldn't even reassure him. Tonight there was no pretense in her.

He nodded then. He turned and filled the glass with smooth economical movements. "That'll be three-fifty."

"I'll just start a tab." The words came unbidden, programmed from years of practicing this art. Her heart quailed. She fumbled with her purse, but her hands were shaking so hard she couldn't even open her wallet. When she looked up the bartender had already turned away. She put the purse down on the counter with a sigh and grabbed on to the beer with both hands.

The glass was cool beneath her fingers. The smell of yeast rose up to taunt her. Beer wasn't her drink of choice, but she'd long ago acquired a taste for anything with alcohol.

A man jostled her elbow. She turned, and he gave her an apologetic shrug. "Sorry, lady."

"It's okay."

"What's a pretty lady like you doing in a dump like this?" As the stranger repeated the age-old line, his thirty-something face changed. Suddenly all she could see was the haggard, filthy man from her past. His breath was foul as he panted in her face. She knew she was naked, except for a residue of vomit on her perspiring skin.

"You're such a pretty girl," the man in her head crooned.

Roxy lurched away, spilling her beer all over the bar.

"Hey, what are you doing?" the thirty-something man asked as he pushed her purse out of the way and then tried to mop up the flowing river of beer with a stack of napkins.

Roxy watched for a moment, breathing fast, she put a hand on her chest. *I can't breathe.* She counted, trying to orient herself in the present.

The man looked up at her. "You could help me with this."

The bartender arrived with soothing words and a rag. As Roxy watched her breathing loosened. She angled away from the thirty-something man who'd wiped up the beer. She gazed over the wooden bar at the various neon signs above it.

One was neon green.

The bartender handed her another beer without prompting.

She opened her purse.

"Don't worry, it's on the house. Hey, are you feeling all right?"

Roxy looked from his concerned expression to the neon green. The beer sat inches from her fingers. She could smell it. She picked up the beer and put it to her lips. She held it there a long moment. The glass stayed level. She licked her lips, waiting for the craving. It came, but it wasn't a howling need. It was somehow diminished, almost manageable. She put the beer on the counter.

She shook her head. "I feel fine. It's just that I'm in the wrong place."

"Are you looking for a particular bar? I know the area."

She smiled and glanced up at the neon sign. "I used to know the area, too."

"All right then. If you're sure you're okay..."

"I'm okay," she told the curious bartender. "I'm finally okay."

If I go back to Luke, maybe I'm just trading one obsession for another. He might become a crutch.

It wouldn't be a great basis for a relationship.

But she didn't think she wanted a crutch. Hadn't she tested the depth of her soul? And instead of falling headlong into the beer she'd discovered the will to resist. The water of her soul wasn't pure, but it wasn't dark, either. Did she dare to reach deeper? For love?

"Something wrong with the beer?" the obviously puzzled bartender asked her.

"I don't need a beer. I think I need to go home."

"You want me to call you a cab?"

She shook her head. "I know the way home."

The bartender nodded and then turned to another customer. She pushed the beer away. Then she rubbed her hand along the smooth, sticky surface of the bar.

She knew the craving for a drink wouldn't go away just because she was going to Luke. She was still bringing him her problems. But she was stronger than she'd thought she was, and tonight she'd proved something to herself. He wouldn't be a crutch. She didn't need Luke. She just wanted him really, really badly.

He can't keep me safe from this problem, but he can love me, and then I'll be even stronger because of our love.

Her lips curved into a smile. She looked at the green neon for the last time. Then leaving a few dollars on the counter, she grabbed her purse and pushed away from the bar. She walked away with a confidence she'd never known before. She was going home.

Roxy walked into the cooling night air, the breeze blowing her hair back from her face. She nearly collided with a very tall man. Suddenly she was looking up into deep brown eyes. "Luke!"

He grabbed her hard. She pushed her face into his chest, breathing him in.

"How did you find me?"

He only let go with one arm. "You left a very cryptic note on your door for someone named Sandra and a bright yellow beacon right outside this bar." He gestured toward her Porsche.

When she'd come she'd thought the fact there was a parking spot open directly in front of the bar was bad luck. It meant she wouldn't have time to change her mind on the walk to the bar. Now she knew it was the best luck of all. Luke had found her. "What do you know," she mused.

He pushed her just far enough away from him to look into her eyes. "What are you doing down here? Is Mick in trouble again?"

Bless him for not assuming she'd been drinking. He would always think the best of her and she would try never to disappoint him.

She shook her head. "I was in trouble. You're just in time to see how this plays out."

His grip tightened infinitesimally. "Are you okay?"

"Don't you mean, am I sober? Would you still want me if I'd fallen off of the wagon?"

His face flushed. "I want you any way I can get you!"

"Then you'll be happy to know I've given in to temptation."

He looked confused and worried. "What do you mean?"

"Don't worry, I didn't drink a drop. I figure alcohol addiction is something I'll just have to endure. But a life without you is absolutely not an option. I plan to feed my addiction to you on a daily basis." She looked into his strong, handsome face. "I'm coming home."

He closed his eyes. When he opened them they were

decidedly moist. "We don't have to live in West Texas. I'd be happy wherever you park your Porsche."

She smiled up at him. "And what would the sheriff of Red Wing do in Dallas?"

"He might get his degree in Archeology, and study some of those Indian relics." He shrugged. "I've got some money saved."

She reached up to touch his face. "I have it on good authority that you've got a whole town counting on you to tuck them in at night. I say we try this sheriff thing. I'll apply to teach. If they can't stomach me, then we'll try something else. In the meantime you can have some archeologists come dig in your precious riverbank. Since you'll be funding the dig, you can be in on all the interesting finds, without having to sit in a classroom."

"How will I fund a dig?"

"You're marrying a girl with a sizable trust fund. What else could we do with all that money in Red Wing, Texas?"

"Are you asking me to marry you?"

This time her smile almost split her face. She knew she would spend the rest of her life thanking God for getting her through hard times, and bringing her to Red Wing and this incredible man. "You're damn right I'm asking you to marry me, and it would be pretty stupid of you to refuse a trust fund!"

He pushed back a curl falling over her ear. "That's what I love about you. You're feisty."

She ran her finger up his chest, wishing they weren't

standing in the middle of a public sidewalk. "Is that the only reason?"

His face flushed. "I can think of lots of others."

"So you've decided?"

"I think you'll have to convince me."

She pulled his head down and whispered in his ear.

His eyes widened and he scooped her off her feet. As she looked up she noticed that even in Dallas there were stars shining down on them.

"How long do you think it will take us to drive to Vegas?"

"It depends on whether or not we use your patrol car." She snuggled against him as he paused in front of her car. He hesitated and his grip tightened as if he didn't want to let her go.

"To hell with it," he said dropping the keys into her lap. He raised the arm under her legs and awkwardly hailed a cab. A cab slowed and Roxy grinned at Luke. "You do have a habit of leaving my car behind."

He nodded. "Yeah, we'll come back for it. We're flying to Vegas. We're going to get married and then we're going to find a motel where we can try what you just described, in bed, in detail, and more than once."

In that moment, she discovered that profound joy was intoxicating, and she looked forward to being addicted for the rest of her life. "Sheriff, I knew I'd corrupt you."

He strode forward toward the cab. "Thank goodness you did," he told her fervently, as he deposited her gently in the back seat of the cab.